PEARL

MAIL ORDER BRIDE TALES

MCDANIEL, SYLVIA

VIRTUAL BOOKSELLER

The Single Father and the Teacher

Jesse McIntire is determined to protect his young daughter from the fate of his late wife. His father sends for a woman to take over his daughter's academic training as well as her feminine etiquette. Jesse refuses to bow down to his father's wishes. Until he sees the beautiful and elegant teacher exit the train... She just might be what his daughter needs–and what he desires.

Dreaming of independence and self-worth that don't require her to be shackled to any man, Pearl Weare denies her attraction to the rugged cowboy. But once she starts falling hard for the Colorado rancher, she must decide between what her heart wants and her convictions.

Can she give her heart to the man who teaches her about home and family, while still holding firm to her beliefs?

CHAPTER 1

*P*earl Weare heard the clink of the jail cell doors and prepared herself for the storm about to erupt. Stepping into the waiting room, her father approached her, his face taut with barely concealed rage. He'd been angry with her before, but she knew there would be consequences for her actions today.

He took her by the arm. "Don't say a word until we're in the carriage."

The building door swung open and several reporters from the Boston Evening Traveler greeted them. "Miss Weare, do you think your father's bank treats women unfairly?"

"Miss Weare, why don't you go to work in your father's bank?"

"Mr. Weare, what do you think of your daughter's involvement in the suffragette movement?"

Her father gripped her elbow, almost dragging her to the waiting carriage. He didn't say a word and she knew from his rigid body, he was the angriest she'd ever seen him. When they reached the buggy, he opened the door and she crawled in, followed closely by her father.

The driver clicked to the horses and away they went with the reporters laughing.

She sighed. She knew better than to say anything. Long ago, she'd learned that nothing embarrassing or revealing was discussed when a servant was nearby. She glanced out the window at the passing homes, knowing her activities with the ladies would be curtailed. Eight long months and then she could walk out of her family home and hopefully into the school she wanted to create for young girls.

The carriage came to a halt in the prosperous neighborhood on Beacon Street. She saw reporters milling around the front of the house close to the street. The door opened and her father waited, holding out his hand. She had no choice, though she wanted nothing more than to escape to her room and avoid the confrontation she knew awaited.

The reporters made a mad dash across the street. "Miss Weare, Miss Weare."

Taking her elbow her father pulled her toward the steps leading into the house. Reluctantly she followed, feeling like she was walking to the gallows. Their maid opened the door. "Good evening, Mr. Weare, Miss Weare."

"Good evening, Bertha," her father said.

Pearl nodded, but kept her lips closed, knowing what was expected of her.

Not releasing her elbow, he took her straight into his office and closed the door.

"Sit," he commanded.

She took a seat in the chair across from him as he went behind his desk. The ticktock of the clock could be heard, but nothing else as they sat staring at one another.

"If your mother were alive, she'd be quite disappointed in you."

Pearl knew better than to argue, and she didn't believe his statement. Her mother had been the one who encouraged her

3

not to define her life by marriage, but rather to learn and grow. And she had, in honor of her mother and then slowly for herself. But she knew better than to talk back. It didn't really matter what she said because her father didn't listen.

"While I'm glad it wasn't my bank you marched against, it's still my competitor."

Next weekend they were slated to march against her father's bank. And she'd known there was no way she could be seen protesting with the women, so she'd gone this weekend. But she wasn't about to tell her father his was on the schedule.

"Attending college was the worst thing I've agreed to. Since you graduated, you've become involved in this women's movement. You've embarrassed the family, my business, and we have reporters in front of our home. I should have married you off years ago."

He sighed and gazed at her. "In your own best interests, I'm sending you out of town for a while until this scandal dies down."

"No," she cried, knowing she wasn't supposed to speak, but unable to stop the word from coming out of her mouth.

He frowned at her. "Silence."

She couldn't be sent away from Boston. She was working with the ladies to find a location for her to start a boarding school to teach young women. They were to look at property next week, and after she received her trust fund in February, she would have the school ready by next fall. There was much to prepare if she wanted to start on time.

"Your aunt told me that Cal McIntire is searching for a teacher for his granddaughter, Grace McIntire. You know, the little girl your cousin had with the rancher from Colorado."

Cousin Beth was the girl who should have been her father's child. She was the one who enjoyed parties and shopping and dancing the night away. She was the one who flirted with every available man and had gotten caught in more than one compromising position. Until she'd eloped with the rancher from Colorado shocking them all. A rancher hadn't seemed the right fit for her.

"I have your train ticket to Denver. You're leaving with your aunt Edwina in the morning."

Pearl shook her head; she couldn't help it. "No, I refuse to go. I'm not going."

Her father shrugged and that concerned her. "Fine. You can stay here, but I will insist you marry."

"No. I'm not getting married."

"Your husband will have control of your trust fund," he said, ignoring her outburst. He leaned back and sighed. "Pearl, it's only until February when you will turn twenty-one and then you can return and claim your trust fund. Then if you want to build a school for suffragettes, I won't stop you. But you have to go to Colorado."

"Why do you want to send me away?"

"Have you looked outside at the reporters? Do you think I want this scandal to reach your younger sister?"

Pearl sighed. Anna was her father's darling. The child of his second marriage and her stepmother would like nothing better than to rid herself of Pearl's presence in the house.

"If I go, I will receive my trust fund in February, free and clear?"

"Of course. And your aunt will go as far as Chicago with you. Then she's leaving us to marry."

Her stepmother must be somewhere in the house dancing right now. She'd be rid of Pearl and Edwina. The house would now only inhabit her children and Pearl's father.

"All right. I'll go, but I'll be back in February and then I will receive my trust fund, and nothing will stop me from building my boarding school."

PEARL STARED out the window of the rocking train, her eyes peering at the lush green countryside that soothed her troubled soul. The rolling mountains, the swaying grass, and the Douglas fir trees dotted the landscape like a living painting.

Part of her wanted to enjoy the beautiful hills and valleys while the defiant part still rebelled. An ache in the center of her chest radiated the hurt and anger that filled her at having been sent away only days after graduating with a degree in teaching from Boston University. All her plans destroyed by her father's objections.

"We're almost there," Aunt Edwina said, patting her on the arm. "Are you nervous?"

She glanced at her aunt, raising her brows. "No. Why should I be? They're getting a well-trained teacher for one student. One student instead of my own boarding school."

After the "incident" her father refused to help her fund a school for young girls. Part of her doubted he would ever help her obtain the funding she needed. He'd resisted her attending college, he'd resisted her becoming a teacher, and he'd become enraged at her involvement with the National Women's Movement.

"In time, dear. Once you receive your money, you can open your school and train young women to become suffragettes. Though I worry many families will keep their children at home once they learn what you're teaching."

Her curriculum would not have been specifically listed as enlightening young women, but she would have infused in them the ability and the hope that they could become more than just wives and mothers. They could become strong, independent women.

"That's why I won't advertise we're training their daughters to think on their own. To learn how to take care of themselves and earn a decent living without depending on a man."

Her aunt shook her head. "I don't know what you have

against men, dear. They're very nice. And if you get a good one, you can soon have them fawning all over you and offering you the best possible life."

Pearl gave an unladylike snort. "Yes, Auntie, I certainly saw that in Chicago. Let's see, you traveled halfway across the continent to learn your beau found someone else or am I not remembering this correctly?"

In Chicago, as the train whistle blew its last warning, Pearl had seen her aunt running as fast as her short legs would carry her toward the train cab. She'd been shocked when Edwina joined her on the journey to Russell Gulch, Colorado.

A scowl drew her aunt's brows together. "No need to be impertinent. That scalawag forgot to mention he had a wife. A new wife."

A giggle escaped from between Pearl's lips. She held it in as long as possible. "A very upset wife that didn't like his fiancée arriving from Boston. How did she find out about you?"

Sighing, her aunt shook her head. "I don't know. At least he met me on the platform to let me know he'd married someone else. I'm glad I learned of his deceit before your train left. That poor porter was dragging my trunk trying to reach the baggage car in time. Now let's hope your cousin Elizabeth's husband isn't upset there are two of us arriving."

It was a concern since he'd only sent for one governess to teach his daughter about being a young girl in a wild frontier city.

"I'll tell him you were jilted at the train station and had no choice but to continue the journey with me."

Her aunt shook her carefully coiffed hair. "I'm only staying until I see you settled. Then I'm continuing on to California. I need a new start. A new place where I can find friends that I enjoy without your father giving them all the evil eye. Or your stepmother raging at me to leave."

More like sisters than aunt and niece, they shared their

woman still clung to the old values and ideas of what a woman should or should not do. And yet, she was protective of Pearl.

"Well, that's a shame, because I would think they would need a strong woman to survive and take charge here in the wilderness. I think this couldn't be a better place for a suffragette movement. But you can rest easy knowing I won't be here long enough to start one. My twenty-first birthday comes in eight months and I'll be gone before next spring."

"If not sooner," Aunt Edwina replied, grabbing her carpet bag as the train came to a halt.

JESSE MCINTIRE GLANCED over in the wagon at Grace who sat between his father Cal and himself. He didn't want to think of his little girl growing up and becoming like her mother. She didn't need to learn how to be a society lady. In Russell Gulch, there was no need for airs or fancy ball gowns or even fancy schooling and yet he wanted his daughter to know how to take care of herself.

"So, Pa, why are we picking up this lady?" she asked, raising her innocent gaze to his.

Those beautiful eyes gave him unconditional love and he wanted to keep it that way. He could raise his daughter without the help of a woman. But his father had different ideas about his granddaughter. He had different ideas about parenting.

"Ask your grandfather," he said, maneuvering the wagon around a hole in the middle of the muddy road. The snow had melted, but the roads had yet to dry. Soon it would be time to thin out the herd and decide which cows went to market. They'd just finished branding all the new spring calves, but still had fence line that needed repairing and a new barn to build before the fall. And now a new governess for Grace. Just what he didn't want to deal with during the busiest time of the year.

At seven years of age, his daughter was growing fast, and he knew the time for her to become a proper young woman would soon be upon them, but still, he wanted to keep her his little girl for as long as possible. He doubted he would have other children. Right now, his daughter was all gangly limbs, blond hair, and sapphire eyes that melted his heart when she gazed at him.

"It's simple enough I can understand, Grace, but your pig-headed father doesn't want to admit you're growing up. You're becoming a young lady. And you need to know how a young girl acts. Your father and I can't help you with that. Neither one of us are girls."

Flashing his father an agitated glance, Jesse didn't want to talk about his daughter becoming a young woman. She was a child. His child.

His daughter's forehead crinkled. "But I don't want to change. I don't want to be like those girls we see at church every Sunday. I want to ride and learn to rope and soon I'll be able to help you and Pa when you're working with the cattle. I don't like dresses."

His father raised his brows, sending Jesse that look that clearly said *this is why your daughter needs a governess. Someone to teach her to be a girl.*

But he wasn't ready to concede just yet. "And you will. You're going to be the best young woman in Colorado who knows how to ride the range and deal with the cattle."

"And, Lord, she'll be the talk of the town," his father said beneath his breath just as they hit a rut in the road.

"What did you say, Grandpa?" Grace asked, turning her innocent young face to his father.

"I said, 'and, Lord, she'll be a great cattle woman,'" he said, shaking his head.

Jesse would rather the town talk about how his daughter rode like a man than for them to discuss how she was spoiled and wore fancy clothes and held silly balls. They didn't need that here in Russell Gulch.

His wife had never fit into the social circle in the little community because she'd always longed for more. He'd warned her when they married that he lived in the wilderness, his ranch five miles from a town of fewer than one hundred people. But somehow the beauty had convinced him she'd love living on a cattle spread.

"What's this lady going to give me lessons on?" the child asked, staring at him with her mother's eyes. He'd fallen in love with those beautiful sapphire eyes and his daughter's were a reflection of her mother's. But a ranch hadn't been a good fit for a woman from the upper class in Boston. And no matter how much he'd loved Beth, it hadn't been enough.

"She's going to instruct you on how to read and write and the proper manners a young girl should know," his father replied.

"But I don't want to learn that stuff. I like learning from you, Grandpa," she said, gazing at him.

His father chuckled. "I've taught you as much as I know. Now it's time for someone else to take over. Especially since there's no school in town."

"I'm sure there was someone local who could have taught Grace," Jesse said, letting his father know he wasn't happy that he'd gone behind his back to bring this woman here.

The town had yet to hire a teacher, so most people were instructing their children at home. His father had been working with Grace. She knew her alphabet, could do more math than most girls, and could read. Jesse wanted her to know more, but the thought of a woman teaching his daughter frightened him.

"I doubt she stays long," Jesse said, thinking he would be doing everything possible to put this woman on the next train heading to Denver. And out of their lives permanently. His daughter could learn from a local woman here in town.

Someone who wouldn't teach her how to act coy with men or flirt, bat her eyelashes or simper with a fan.

No, his daughter would never be an outrageous flirt like her mother. No woman was going to show his daughter how to tempt a man.

As the buggy pulled into Denver, they saw the train in the distance.

"Pa, have you ever ridden a train?"

"Yes, I have. I once went all the way to Boston," he said.

"That's where you met Mother?" the little girl questioned.

"Yes," he said, sighing, remembering how enamored he'd been of the city and his wife, but longed to come home to the open spaces, eagles floating in the sky, and the breeze blowing through the firs.

"Someday I want you to take me to Boston. I'd like to see where Mother lived."

Jesse was silent. He'd never take his child to visit Boston because he didn't want his wife's family to take an interest in his daughter. It was bad enough Beth's cousin was coming out to teach Grace, but he didn't want her near that family.

"We're getting close to town," he said, changing the discussion, unable to tell his daughter no, but not willing to lie to her either.

He glanced at his father, sending him a frustrated gaze. The old man knew he didn't want his wife's family involved with his daughter. Yet here they were in town picking up her cousin.

His father had said Pearl Weare's father had asked if she could come teach Grace while he searched for a husband for her. He wanted to get his daughter out of Boston for a while. Was there a reason she'd needed to leave the city and why would any man send his daughter across the country without a chaperone?

Was she really here to teach his daughter or try to steal her away?

His hands clenched around the reins at the thought of someone trying to take his daughter, his insides churning with rage. He didn't care how rich his dead wife's family was. They would have one hell of a fight on their hands if they thought they could lure or take his daughter.

Sometimes the old man just didn't think things through and by agreeing to let Miss Weare come to the ranch, he was afraid her family wanted Grace.

He pulled the wagon to a halt. "Here we are. Let's go see about your new teacher."

CHAPTER 2

*P*earl followed her aunt off the train, stepping onto the platform. The mountain air had her taking a deep breath and releasing it slowly. She wasn't in Boston anymore. They hurried to where the men were unloading their trunks.

"Have you seen them?" Edwina asked.

"I have no idea what they look like. I expected to be picked up by two men and a little girl."

"Well, you look while I find our trunks."

This was not how she'd planned on spending her summer. She'd been in negotiations to purchase a large house with the potential to become her boarding school when her father announced she'd be spending time in Colorado—clear across the continent from Boston, the suffragettes, her school, and her dreams.

"Excuse me, are you Miss Weare?" a tall gentleman asked, wearing a cowboy hat that shaded his handsome face from the sun. The man's legs were long, lean, his chest was firm, his shoulders broad and his arms muscled. For a moment, she caught herself staring, then quickly glanced into his eyes, knowing instinctively that this was her cousin's widower.

"Yes," she said breathlessly, then noticed an older gentleman and little girl with him. The child was dressed in pants and a shirt, with her hair loosely braided.

"Welcome to Denver, miss," the older gentleman said with a welcoming smile. "I'm Calhoun McIntire and this," he said, pushing the girl forward, "is Grace."

She bent down. "Hi, Grace, I'm Pearl, your mother's cousin," she said, gazing at the child knowing that Beth would be appalled at the garb of the beautiful little girl. "I'm here to teach you."

A trickle of unease wound its way down her spine. She'd never taught any children before. Sure, she had a teaching degree, but she planned on being on the other side of education. She'd only wanted to run the school. But now she'd get a first-hand chance of being a teacher.

"I'm Grace's father, Jesse McIntire," the handsome cowboy who'd taken her breath away said to her.

She'd never reacted to a man before, but this one reeked of pure male and she suddenly understood how her flamboyant, irreverent cousin had married him. They had hardly been suitable for each other, but she could see the attraction her cousin must have felt.

"Nice to meet you," she said, wishing Beth were here and she wouldn't be alone with this man she could hardly keep from staring at. With a deep breath, she reminded herself she could do this for eight months.

"Let's get your trunk and then we'll head to Russell Gulch."

"We have to wait for my aunt," she said slowly. "She's gone to find our trunks."

Pearl watched the confusion cross his face.

"Aunt?"

"Your father never mentioned anyone else coming with you," Cal said, stepping forward.

"She wasn't supposed to. The plan was for her to accompany me to Chicago and then for her to stay there, but things didn't work out. She'll be staying a few weeks and then she'll be leaving for California," Pearl replied, hoping they wouldn't object because her aunt was already here, even though part of her realized if they refused to let Edwina stay, it would be her own chance to escape. But right now, she was tired, hungry, dirty and just wanted to rest before she tackled changing the world.

Her aunt strolled up to the group. "Hello, I'm Miss Edwina Weare. So nice to meet you all."

Her bubbly effervescence seemed to lighten the mood and Pearl watched the two men exchange a glance over the top of the girl's head. "I'm so sorry to be intruding, but I hadn't planned on being jilted at the train station. One moment I'm engaged to be married and the next I learned he already has a wife. So here I am."

Inside, Pearl cringed at her aunt's remarks. The woman didn't know how to keep a secret. She didn't know that every stranger she met didn't want her life story and all her troubles. She didn't know that sometimes less was better.

Grace tugged on her father's pants. He glanced down at her. "Pa, what is jilted?"

"It means rejected," he said softly.

The little girl frowned. "What's rejected?"

Her aunt squatted down to the girl. "You must be Grace."

"Yes, ma'am."

"Well, Grace, rejected means he didn't want to marry me."

"Oh," the girl said.

"It can happen with arranged marriages," Edwina said more to herself than the little girl as she stood and glanced at the men. "And your names are?"

The older gentleman stepped forward. "Sorry, I got a little too wrapped up in your tale. I'm Calhoun McIntire and this is my son Jesse."

"I'll only be staying long enough to see my niece settled, then I'll be going to California."

From the looks on the men's faces, Pearl wasn't certain they wanted her to stay for two weeks. No, it wasn't what they'd planned, but she wasn't about to leave her aunt in a perilous situation. The woman managed to find those on her own.

Jesse nodded. "We have a small house on the property that was our original homestead before I built our current home. You two ladies can stay out there together. You'll be safe."

"Splendid," Edwina said and took Pearl by the arm. "Our trunks are sitting right over there. Grace, why don't you lead us to the wagon."

"Okay," the young girl said as she strode across the platform in her pants and boots.

If Beth were still alive, her daughter would not be running around looking like a little boy. No, in fact, Beth had always been the frilly feminine dresser. The one who had the latest fashions and wore the latest designs.

Pearl had been shocked when she'd heard she was marrying and moving to Colorado. She'd never thought of her cousin as someone who would enjoy living in the wilderness.

At the wagon, Jesse took Pearl's arm and helped her in. The feel of his hand in hers sent a jolt of awareness through her that made her jump as warmth spread into her limbs. Now was not the time for her to start thinking of men and marriage. She had a school to build.

Taking a seat on a hard, wooden bench, she realized the wagon wasn't a nice buggy like the one back home. Shaking herself, she had to stop thinking that way. She wasn't in Boston any longer and she doubted she would ever return to her home.

"We better hurry if we're going to make it to the cabin before dark."

"Cabin? I thought you have a house," Pearl said. "A ranch."

"I do, but it's a two-day wagon ride from here."

She glanced at Edwina whose eyes were wide as saucers. "What? Where will we sleep."

"Oh, don't worry, there's a real nice cabin we all sleep in together. You'll see," Grace informed them.

They would be staying in a cabin, overnight? With two men they barely knew?

Uneasiness trickled down Pearl's spine.

Jesse glanced back and smiled. "You ladies will sleep in the cabin. Pa and I, we'll sleep out in the wagon."

The man was enjoying her unease. She glanced around the town of Denver.

"You don't have a stagecoach in Russell Gulch?"

Cal laughed. "No, ma'am, we're a ranching, mining community with a mercantile and a church to make us appear civilized."

Pearl sighed. Her father had found a remote area to send her to, away from the crowds, the suffragettes and no way to access her trust fund. He might as well have banished her from society.

THE SCENERY LIFTED Pearl's spirits as the wagon bounced along the dusty road. The distant mountains were topped with snow and then sloped down to luscious green meadows filled with cattle. The land was untarnished and the sight of a cabin or a home was rare.

After the long train ride, the clean fresh air was like a balm to her tired soul. Four days bouncing on a train had left her beyond exhausted and she feared her body would never be the same. Then there had been the drama of Aunt Edwina continuing the journey with her and now the excitement of finally arriving in Denver only to discover they had a multi-day wagon trip to reach Russell Gulch.

Not to mention spending the night in a cabin on the side of the road. She didn't know which was worse, the motion of the train or the jarring bounce of the wagon. And frankly, she was ready to reach her destination and rest. To lie flat and not move.

At first, they had chatted nonstop about the trip, Grace asking her all kinds of questions, but soon the choking dust and the jerking of the wagon had silenced everyone. Now, shadows were lengthening, and she was ready to be motionless for a little while.

"There it is, Pa," Grace said, sitting between her father and grandfather.

"I see it, Grace," Jesse said, smiling down at his daughter. "I think you're ready to get out for a while."

"Yes," she said.

"I can't say that I blame you," her grandfather replied. "And my stomach is reminding me we haven't eaten in a while."

Jesse pulled the wagon up to the cabin and glanced around. "Ladies, it's not the nicest place, but it will have to do. I'll carry your trunks inside."

"What kind of building is this?" Edwina asked.

Cal glanced back at her and grinned. "It's the Colorado version of a way station. There are several along the road to Denver. It's a place to spend the night out of the cold and weather."

Just then the rumble of thunder resounded in the mountains. "Sounds like we're in for a little rain," Jesse said, looking at the sky. "Sorry, ladies, but I think we're all going to sleep in the cabin tonight."

"Absolutely not," Edwina said. "It's not proper."

Cal climbed out of the wagon, reached back and lifted Grace out, then he turned to Edwina. He placed his hands around her waist and lifted her from the wagon. "You think we should bed down here in the back of the wagon in the rain with the temperature falling while you're all snuggly warm in the cabin?"

She frowned. "Maybe we could put up a blanket. One side for the men and one for the women."

"Maybe, but frankly, I'd rather use that blanket to wrap around my body and keep me warm."

Edwina looked down her nose at him and raised her brows. "Looks to me like you've got plenty of muscle to keep you warm."

Cal roared with laughter. "Miss Weare, you're right. But the cold still seeps in. You'll soon see."

"Boston has plenty of cold nights."

A rumble of thunder had Jesse glancing at the sky. He reached up to help Pearl alight from the wagon. His hands felt warm around her waist. "There is a creek for water and a privy around back. I wouldn't wait since we could be in for a night of rain. I'll unload everything and feed the horses. Then I'll be in to warm up our supper."

"I'll take the bags in, Pa," Grace said, grabbing several cases that were almost as big as her.

"Whoa, girl, let me help you," her grandfather said, taking the bags that Grace was dragging into the cabin.

The little girl shrugged and let him have them while Jesse unharnessed the horses from the wagon and ground tethered them.

"Come on, I'll show you the privy," Grace said, skipping out of the cabin.

Glancing around, Pearl and Edwina followed her to the back. There they found a circle of rocks...their toilet. Edwina glanced at Pearl. "I knew I should have hopped back on that train and headed to San Francisco. But oh no, I was worried about you and decided to stay."

Pearl laughed as another rumble of thunder sounded closer.

"I think we better get back to the cabin or find ourselves getting wet."

A few minutes later, the three girls came back around the side of the little building as it started to rain. Opening the door, Pearl stepped in and saw where they would spend the night.

She smiled and reminded herself that her father was punishing her. But she would never let him know how his discipline had affected her. Right now, even sleeping on that narrow straw mattress with no sheets was better than the constant rumble of the train. And she had to remember the outcome of this adventure would lead to her receiving her trust fund.

"Oh, dear," Edwina said, getting her first glance at the bunks in the corner. "I take dibs on the lower one."

Pearl didn't know if she was beyond exhausted, but the look on her aunt's face sent her into a spasm of giggles. When she finally stopped laughing, she glanced at her aunt watching her. "What have I done?"

❧

STANDING OUTSIDE under the overhang of the cabin's eaves, Jesse watched the storm roll over the top of the mountain, then sink down into the valley toward them. Thunder rumbled in the craggy tops.

He knew that a thunderstorm in June could bring not only a torrential downpour, but even hail or sleet. If the lightning became bad enough, he'd bring the horses into the cabin with them.

But in the wilderness, a man's horse was his mode of transportation and you protected your animal at all costs. Even at the expense of your own comfort.

His father stepped outside and joined him. "What's the weather like?"

"I'm watching it. If it gets serious, I won't hesitate to bring the horses into the house."

His father laughed. "That would set off those women from Boston."

"Better to set them off than to tell them we're walking the rest of the way to Russell Gulch."

Jesse could see both Pearl and Edwina probably fainting at the sight of a couple of horses in a cabin. "You've got a point."

Just then lightning crackled across the evening sky and thunder rumbled, echoing in the mountains. "I got a fire going in the cabin to knock the chill out of the air. And there's a basket of cold fried chicken we can have for supper."

"That's better than going hungry."

When he'd set Miss Weare on the ground after lifting her from the wagon, he'd seen the distain in her eyes. The woman came from a family in Boston that had that new indoor plumbing.

He doubted she knew how to start a fire and probably had never cooked a day in her life. She would be in for a rude surprise when she realized she would be using an outhouse and expected to cook her own breakfast and lunch.

Beth had hated living at Russell Gulch. She'd hated Colorado and eventually she'd hated Jesse. He didn't expect anything different from her cousin.

"I thought in the morning we could have some cold biscuits and beef jerky before we started for home."

Jesse looked at his father. Even though he was grown with a child of his own, his father made certain they all had enough to eat.

"Thanks, I'd forgotten all about breakfast. So, what do you think of Miss Weare? Are you still certain she can teach Grace?"

"I have no doubts our girl is about to get an education. And I think she's going to teach you a thing or two."

Jesse made a *phew* noise with his mouth. "What would she teach me?"

Beth had schooled him well in marriage and he wanted nothing more to do with women. He had his family, his daughter, and the land he loved. He didn't need anything else, though his father kept encouraging him to give women a second chance. He knew they could be fun, but he liked his life. It was peaceful and quiet, and no one was complaining they didn't have any parties to attend.

"That women are not all the same and your daughter will eventually become one of them, no matter how much you try to stop her from growing."

"I know Grace is going to become a woman. But she's still a little girl and I want her to remain one for as long as possible."

His father's comments were ridiculous. He knew his daughter was going to eventually grow up, but she would be well schooled in how to live in Colorado and she would know how to take care of herself and the ranch they both loved.

His father shook his head. "We should have gone by the mercantile while we were in town and bought her new clothes. She needs a dress."

"My daughter has two dresses and chooses to wear pants. I'm just fine with what she wears."

Cal leaned against a post, folded his arms across his chest and sighed. "Don't you remember when you were eight and that kid Jonah made fun of you because your shirttail was ripped."

"Of course, I remember," Jesse said, gazing at his father. "I dealt with it. I think I gave him a black eye. And Mick ripped his shirt."

"Your mother overheard the boy and she went through all of your clothes, making certain that none of them had rips and tears. She felt it was her fault, and honestly, I think she wanted to paddle that kid for being so rude."

To this day, Jesse still missed his mother. While he remembered the kid making fun of him, he didn't know that his mother had gone through his clothing. Ida had been a caring, gentle woman who took care of those she loved until the day she died.

"How does this apply to Grace?" he asked.

"There's going to come a day when the kids will pick on her for looking different."

"And I'll beat the tar out of any of them that do," he said, gazing out at the landscape. The rain was easing up and even the thunder seemed to be drifting away.

His father laughed. "No matter how much you resist it, Grace is going to grow up."

"And when she's ready to accept being a girl or woman, then I will as well. Until then, she's free to wear what she wants."

"You have a stubborn streak equal to your mother's. I wish that Mick would come home."

His brother Mick had left Colorado to join a wild west show. They hadn't heard from him in months. They were worried about him, but couldn't do much since he was an adult.

"Thank you. Now let's go in before they eat all the chicken. I think the storm has calmed enough that the horses are safe."

"Jesse, someday I hope you find real love. The kind I had with your mother."

He'd wanted a marriage like his parents and thought he'd found that with Beth, but then he'd quickly learned differently. Now he wanted to work his ranch and watch his daughter grow. He didn't need a woman or marriage.

"Let's go in, Pa," he said roughly, wishing his mother was still here.

CHAPTER 3

*T*he next day, they arrived at the ranch, exhausted after a two-day journey in the wagon. His housekeeper Florence had supper simmering when they arrived, and after he'd shown the ladies their house, they sat to eat.

Jesse watched Pearl all evening. The woman was poised. She was graceful, she was quiet and listened intently to Grace, but she didn't act like she'd been around children much and that surprised him.

If a woman were a teacher, one would think she'd know children, but Pearl seemed more reserved. Maybe she was tired. After all, he'd made that train trip before, and at the end, one felt like they'd been in a bar fight from all the rocking, jolting, and sitting.

They were gathered in the family room, the parlor much too fancy for his liking, and someday soon, he was going to tear down all the frilly decorations Beth had insisted on in that room. He looked at his daughter. "It's bed time, young lady. You start working with Miss Weare tomorrow and you need your sleep."

Grace glanced at everyone in the room. "No one else is going to bed."

"We'll all be right behind you. I'm going to talk to Miss Weare about your curriculum and then I'll be climbing the stairs. The two ladies are staying at the homestead, so they'll be leaving as well."

Slowly she stood. She went first to her grandfather and then to her father and kissed them each on the cheek. "Goodnight."

His daughter was precious to him and he loved her more than he thought possible. Yes, he probably spoiled her, but her life was here in Colorado and he never wanted her to leave.

Her family in Boston would have to pry her from his cold, dead arms if they thought of taking her away. So the high and mighty teacher they'd sent could return on the next train as far as he was concerned. And he intended to let her know in no uncertain terms that his daughter would never leave.

"Be sure to brush your teeth," he called as she climbed the stairs to her room.

"I'll be up in a few minutes to say prayers with you."

"Okay, Pa. Goodnight, everyone."

The woman, Pearl, was sitting close to the fire, her burnished hair shined brightly in the firelight and her brown eyes watched everything. He'd sat as far from her as possible at dinner, afraid of the attraction he felt toward this gorgeous woman. He wasn't going to get involved with another woman. Especially from the Weare family and Boston.

With reluctance, he rose from his chair. Better get this over with so they could all retire for the night. "Miss Weare, let's go to my office and talk for a few minutes."

"Of course," she said, rising from the rocker close to the fire.

He led her down the hallway to his favorite room in the house where he shut the door behind her when she entered. He pointed to a seat and then went behind the desk where he sank into the leather chair his wife had purchased for him years ago.

"Your home is lovely. I can see some touches of Beth in different areas."

They were memories of why he would never marry again. Memories that his first wife had hated living in Colorado, hated the house he'd built for her and thought the ranch was a rustic reclusive dreadful place. He doubted many in her family knew she'd left him for the bright lights and fancy balls in New Orleans. She'd left not only him, but their daughter as well.

He'd sent a letter to her family saying she was visiting in New Orleans, leaving it up to Beth to explain why she wasn't in Colorado where she belonged.

"Yes," he said curtly. "Tell me about your teaching experience."

"I just graduated, so Grace will be my first pupil, but I did have practice at several of the schools in Boston."

Just great. His father had hired a woman who had very little experience in teaching.

"Grace is a delightful child, though she could use some help looking like a little girl," Pearl said.

He frowned. His daughter would not become like her mother and if she wanted to spend the rest of her life dressed like a boy, he'd be just fine. There was no need for the woman to think she was going to change his daughter into one of those pampered misses he'd met in Boston.

"Grace is free to dress however she chooses. Just like you are free to dress the way you wish."

"I'll keep that in mind."

A smile crossed her face which brightened her look and made her appear happier. The young woman was beautiful, and his body reacted to her like a wolf calling for its mate, but he was not heeding the call.

"Mr. McIntire, why did you bring me out here if you don't want your daughter to become more socially acceptable?"

"I didn't bring you," he said. "My father is the one who thinks

28

she should be dressing and acting ladylike. As far as I'm concerned, you can catch the next train back to Denver and forget all about my daughter."

She raised her brows at him in a haughty manner. "Part of me would like to take you up on that offer right now. But I need this job for at least a little while."

So she hadn't come to take his daughter back to Boston? She was from his dead wife's family. Did they not want Grace like he feared?

"Why did you come out here, Miss Weare, if you have no intention on staying long?"

Why would a woman like her come all the way to Colorado with no intention of remaining? None of this made sense to him.

"My father has control of my trust fund and I'm under his rule until the day I receive my inheritance. On that day, we'll have a parting of ways."

She had a trust fund. A woman with a dowry. Why had no eligible society bachelor picked her up at the latest soiree? What was wrong with Miss Weare for her to be so beautiful, an educated teacher, and single?

"And it was your father who insisted you come out here?"

"Yes," she said, not giving any other information. Why had her father insisted she leave Boston? "So you're not here to try to convince my daughter to return with you to where her mother lived or her family?"

The woman tilted her head and gazed at him. "Is that what you thought?"

"It had crossed my mind," he said, staring into the deepest cinnamon eyes he'd ever seen. She was more beautiful than Beth. But she still had that same air about her that said rich city girl.

"If the child was being abused by you or I felt she wasn't receiving the care she needed, then yes, I would pack her up and take her back. But Grace seems happy with you and her grand-father. Her happiness is what's important."

Stunned, he stared at the woman. That sounded so logical, so nurturing, that he didn't know if he could believe her. Time would show if she really believed what she said or if she had other plans.

"What do you want me to teach your daughter while I'm here?" she asked.

He glanced at the young woman, noticing the strong jut of her chin, the way her cheekbones were high, the way her nose tilted on the end, her full very kissable lips. Had she let some man take advantage of her in Boston?

Did she have scandal associated with her name and her father wanted everything to die down before he brought her home? Was she like his first wife, a high-society, snooty young woman?

"I want you to teach Grace what she would learn in any school. I want her to know how to read and write and do math. Give her an understanding of the world, but I don't want my daughter to be turned into a fashionable snob."

Pearl's brows rose. "What is a fashionable snob?

"Your cousin Beth is the perfect example. I don't want my daughter to become like her mother."

PEARL AND EDWINA carried a lantern the short distance to the house. They'd already unpacked most of their belongings, each taking a bedroom. There was even a tiny kitchen with a farm-house sink and a two-burner stove. A parlor held two over-stuffed chairs and a small table where Pearl would teach Grace. She'd already laid out the books she'd brought with her. Tomorrow morning, she would begin.

"Jesse seems like a nice young gentleman. He's a rugged looking man who would fill out a suit very well."

Pearl turned to glance at her aunt but was unable to see her expression in the dark. "Yes, you're right."

"I'm kinda of surprised he didn't walk us to the house."

"What's going to get us? Coyotes?"

Her aunt sighed. "Maybe so. I guess we're used to living in the city."

"Yes, and I think Mr. McIntire would love to take us back to Denver and board us on the next train out of here."

After their discussion, she'd understood the detached aloofness of her employer. He hadn't wanted her to come; his father had hired her.

"What makes you say that?" her aunt asked as they hurried toward the house.

The hoot of an owl sent a tremor down Pearl's spine. Her conversation with Jesse had been revealing. The man may have married her cousin, but it was obvious at this time, he only had disdain for his dead wife. And Pearl wondered what had happened to make him fall out of love with Beth.

"He told me so. He didn't want us to come and teach his daughter. His father did."

"The old man?"

"Yes," Pearl said. A coyote howled in the darkness and something rustled in the brushes off to her right. She shuddered in the cool night air. It wasn't cold, but it certainly wasn't warm either.

The air had a crispness that had her wrapping her shawl around her shoulders a little tighter. They were almost to the house and she couldn't wait to get inside and lock the door.

"Well fiddle dee. Maybe you should just come to San Francisco with me."

A giggle bubbled up inside Pearl at the idea of completely

disobeying her father and taking off with her aunt. The woman her father had no idea had not gotten back on the train in Chicago. His sister, the one he considered wayward and loose with questionable morals because she didn't obey his every word.

"Oh, that would end any chance of me ever getting my inheritance. Father would find some way to keep me from the money, saying I'm incompetent or too wild. He has the connections to make certain I would never see a penny of that money."

They were both silent as they reached the porch and Pearl held open the door for her aunt, shining the light into the house. The woman halted just inside, her body stiffening as she shrieked like she'd seen a bear. Turning, she ran out of the house and down the steps. "Mice! Mice! Lots of mice!"

Pearl peered in the door and shivered at the sight of five mice racing across the floor, scurrying through a crack in the wood and disappearing from sight. Surely, Mr. McIntire didn't expect them to live in a house infested with the furry little creatures? She glanced at her aunt now standing outside the house trembling in the cold night air. "Wait here."

Marching back up to the main house, she entered the home. Silence permeated the living area, the fire dying in the fireplace. Obviously, they'd all gone to bed. She wasn't about to walk to his bedroom.

"Mr. McIntire," she called. "Mr. McIntire," her voice growing louder hoping he wasn't asleep just yet.

A door cracked open and he came to a railing that looked over the main living area and peered down at her. She sucked in a lungful of air, her heart racing at the sight of his broad, naked chest.

She'd never seen the naked male anatomy. She swallowed and looked away. He wasn't decent and yet she wanted another glance at that well-defined chest, his arms thick with muscles.

"Is there a problem," he said with a yawn.

She felt foolish. She licked her lips, knowing how ridiculous she looked standing here and the words she was about to speak would sound like a typical female in distress. Pearl hated appearing weak to any man.

"There are mice in the house."

"Yes, I'm sure there are. We'll set some traps for them in the morning."

"But they're scurrying around in the open. Crawling on..."

Pearl hated sounding like a whiny female needing a man to help her. She was independent and strong and so out of her element in an unknown house. She hated looking up at him, noticing the way his hair was tousled and the grin on his handsome face.

"What do you want me to do? Get my gun and come shoot them?"

The man was her employer for the next eight months. How did she respond nicely to that comment? Her first response would be to tell him politely to yes, bring his gun and shoot the vermin.

It would be nice if he were to give up his sleeping quarters and let her and her aunt occupy a mice free bed, but that could be perilous at the least.

Instead, she took a deep breath, pulled back her shoulders and said, "I expect you to correct this problem in the morning."

"Duly noted, madam," he said with a smirk. "Now, is there anything else you need?"

"No," she replied, knowing she'd made no progress. No help. She had no solution to her dilemma.

"Pleasant dreams, Miss Weare," he said stiffly.

She wanted to smack him, but instead she turned on her heel and walked out the door. The cook from the main house had told her she'd stocked a few food items in the house for them to eat if she got hungry. Pearl would set her own trap. Too bad she didn't have a big enough trap for that annoying man.

ð

JESSE WALKED his daughter down to the house where the ladies had spent their first night. This morning he'd laughed as he remembered the expression on Miss Weare's face when he'd told her the problem could wait until morning. And it could.

It was just mice, not a rattlesnake or a fox or a bear. A small tiny mouse that he'd set a trap for later today and by tomorrow the problem would be handled. One more reason for her to hop on that eastbound train.

This was a perfect example of why the beautiful Miss Weare wouldn't be staying long in Colorado. If a little mouse frightened her, what would she do when she was faced with a grizzly? Faint and become bear food?

Beth never fit in here and the sooner Miss Weare realized this country wasn't for her, the better. Until then, his daughter would get some education.

"I want you to work hard with Miss Weare and do everything she says," he reminded his daughter. "You're a smart little girl and I expect you to do well."

His daughter frowned. "I'd rather go riding with you and Grandpa."

In some ways, he'd rather have her with him where he could keep an eye on her and know for certain her head wouldn't be filled with ideas of parties and belles of the ball and dresses and men. Not his daughter.

"If the weather's nice, we'll go fishing on Saturday. I'm hungry for some trout," he promised his daughter.

A smile brightened her face. Since her mother had left, he'd tried to spend extra time with Grace, taking her with him and not leaving her behind. He was her only parent and she needed him.

"That will be fun." She stopped and glanced up at him, her blue eyes shimmering with tears making his heart ache. But he knew it was in her best interest for her to learn more than he or his father could teach her. "Do I need to learn?"

He wrapped his arm around her. "Education is important. The more you know, the better you understand why things happen. You'll be better prepared in life and that's what I want for you. To learn how to make better decisions. So that you're smarter than me and Grandpa. And it starts with education."

She gazed up at him like he'd lost his mind and he realized he'd probably talked over her head, but hopefully she understood he wanted her to learn. "No one is smarter than you, Pa."

Her words knocked the wind right out of his lungs. His daughter knew just the right thing to say that filled his chest with pride, his heart flooding with love for his little girl.

Blinking the tears from his eyes, he glanced away and gruffly said, "Let's get you there, so you can get started."

"Okay," his daughter said reluctantly, climbing the steps with him.

He knocked on the door and Pearl opened the wooden entrance. "Good morning, Grace, Mr. McIntire."

"Good morning. I trust you slept well."

"Exceptional," she said with a smile.

After she'd returned to the house last night, he'd been afraid she would be upset this morning. He really hadn't expected her to be so cheerful. So happy and eager to get started.

"I'll have one of the men come by later and set out some traps." He really had regretted the way he'd treated her last night. But it was a mouse, and in the scheme of life here in Colorado, they weren't very frightening.

"Wonderful. In the meantime, here," she said and handed him his fish basket. The container he took on his fishing trips and placed his trout in after he'd caught them. Muffled squeals and scratching against the basket in his hands had him glancing at the container and then at Miss Weare.

"What's inside?" he asked and lifted the lid a little.

Inside, six house mice were trying to crawl up the side of the reed bin to escape their fate. His lungs seized for a moment as he stared in surprise at the varmints in the basket and then at Pearl. He'd never expected this. And certainly not six of the rascals. He'd thought she was exaggerating when she'd mentioned more than one.

"You need to make certain the lid is tied down tightly. One of the little buggers escaped this morning by climbing up and sneaking out between the ream of the lid."

He stared at her in awe, wondering how she'd caught them and realizing she'd been right. The house had been infested with mice. A twinge of guilt and regret came over him and he felt bad for not coming down last night and seeing for himself.

"How, did you catch them?" he asked, stunned at what she'd done.

"I found some wire in your barn and I made me a trap. Then I placed a piece of fruit here in the cage and some grain I found. So far I've caught seven, but one got away," she said smiling at him. "Bring back the basket."

The woman was crazy. She'd gone into his barn at night without his men stopping her or ringing the bell alarming everyone that someone was in the barn? What had his men been doing?

"You went out into the barn at night." The house was a ways from the barn and in the darkness, she could have come across a coyote, a fox or even a bear. What in the world had she been doing roaming around in the dark? Probably without a light.

"I took a lantern."

"My men, no one stopped you?" he asked to make certain they'd failed him.

"You were in bed asleep," she said in a way that let him know she'd been put out with him. "And your men? I never saw anyone but the stars and the moon above me."

Jesse sucked in a gulp of breath and let it out slowly. He

didn't want her wandering around at night. Anything could've happened to her.

"Miss Weare, please do not go into the barn after dark, alone. It's not safe and I don't want to see you get hurt," he said, trying not to grit his teeth at his frustration with this woman who had no clue as to where she was living and the dangers around her.

"Fine. But I will not live in a mouse-infested house. I would appreciate it if you would set the necessary traps to get rid of the pesky little animals."

He nodded, knowing he should have taken care of this last night. "I'll have the traps set today."

"Thank you, Mr. McIntire."

"You're welcome, Miss Weare."

"Is there anything else you need besides the mice removed?" he questioned, wanting to make certain that he'd not shirked his duties in any other way.

"No, we're good," she said.

He glanced at his daughter and she was staring at the two of them a strange look on her face, her forehead drawn together like a gathering storm.

"Are you ready to start, Grace?"

"Yes, ma'am."

"Good day, Mr. McIntire. Grace will be finished by two this afternoon."

She opened the door for his daughter and then closed it behind her, shutting him out. The loss of his daughter frightened him for a moment. She was growing up much too quickly and he didn't want her to change.

He cursed beneath his breath, standing there with a fish basket full of mice. For crying out loud, he had to make certain this woman was soon headed back to Boston to her fancy parlors and latest fashions.

But he couldn't deny the woman had grit.

37

CHAPTER 4

*C*alhoun 'Cal' McIntire liked to think of himself as a ladies' man. At least in the last five years he had. When his wife Ida had died, he'd mourned and missed his beautiful bride of almost thirty years.

Not a day went by when he didn't think of her and want to tell her something or kiss her full lips until they were both satisfied. But she was gone, and he was a man who needed the comfort of a woman's touch.

There was something special about the feel of a woman laying her hand on your arm, the caress of her fingertips, or if he was really lucky, kissing her lips.

Yes, Cal liked women and had never hidden that from his wife or his son. Since her death, he'd occasionally gone to town to get a drink in the local saloon, dine with a lady friend, or even visit the boarding house where a man could spend time between the sheets.

He strolled out of the house on his way to the barn, intent on saddling his horse and riding into town to spend some quality time at Dry Gulch Saloon. It had been a while and well, the lovely Miss Edwina McIntire had sparked a fire deep in his belly. It would be in his best interest to have that fire squelched sooner rather than later.

Quickly, he saddled his horse and pulled the spirited mare into the yard. It was then he saw Edwina, sitting on the porch, some kind of needlework in her lap. Never a man to let a beautiful woman sit idle, he pulled his horse down to her.

"Good morning, ma'am. How are you this fine Colorado morning?"

She raised her brows at him. "Not well."

That didn't sound good. "What's wrong?"

Hoping it wasn't one of those female things. Lord, women's pipes could cause more problems than an Indian uprising.

"Rats!" she said with a shudder. "If I had my way, we'd be moving into town into a hotel."

"In the house?" he questioned, watching how the sunlight radiated on her coiffed blond hair. Last night she'd been a delight to watch all evening, making him miss female companionship even more. Making him realize he was lonely.

"Yes. Lots of mice scurrying around like the disgusting creatures they are."

She pushed her needle through the cloth, smoothing the material, her cool emerald eyes assessing him. How did a man respond to Miss Edwina? Last night, she had sat back and assessed them all. She'd flirted some with Jesse, but mainly she'd been analyzing.

"I'll offer a bounty on them," he said softly wanting to provoke her. "Five dollars for every varmint caught inside the old homestead. Bring your gun, hunt big game in the McIntire homestead. Or we could do catch a mouse, kiss a pretty girl. Of course, it's your lips they'd want to kiss, not mine."

Putting her needlework down, she stood and walked to the edge of the porch. How many times had Ida met him there as he rode in from the field? The memory was pleasant and painful at the same time. Yet, this was not Ida. This woman carried herself with refined dignity and he didn't think she appreciated his comments. But that was Cal. He didn't much care.

"Mr. McIntire, I'm certain you're enjoying this at my expense. I'm the one who had to worry about them crawling into bed, if they were getting into my trunk and would continue the journey with me. But most of all, I think you're laughing at me." She walked down the stairs to where his Appaloosa horse stood waiting for him.

Women were such a delight to agitate and this one seemed she could be riled up in less time than it took to fry an egg.

"Yes, ma'am, I think you're right. I am," he said, laughing. "At least we agree that I'm getting a good chuckle out of this."

She narrowed her eyes at him in a way that only women could do that seemed to ignite a fire all the way to a man's groin.

"Oh, Mr. McIntire, you don't want to laugh at a woman like me. I'm not some innocent young girl. I have a tendency to find a way to make a man pay for his entertainment at my expense."

He chuckled. He just bet she could too. "You know, I think I'm going to enjoy your visit. But just remember, I'm not a young man, either, nor do I always stay within polite manners. And I love to bedevil a woman. Especially a beautiful one like yourself. Good day, Miss Edwina. Let me know if you need help catching those mice. I'd prefer the kiss to the five-dollar bounty."

He rode off feeling smug at how he'd gotten to the intriguing Miss Edwina Weare. It was fun to rile a woman like that and watch the color flood her cheeks. It had to be good for the body as it certainly made her even more beautiful than when he'd first seen her.

❧

PEARL KNEW she could teach children. Her professors had given her high marks and told her she would make an excellent administrator or teacher, but for the first time, she could sense her pupil's boredom.

And every time she tried to show her something new, she'd glanced at Pearl with an annoyed look and told her she already knew that. The child wasn't being rude, but so far Pearl had not engaged with the little girl.

Her grandfather had obviously done a great job showing her the basics. Now Pearl needed to spark the child's interest by teaching her something that stretched the limits of her current knowledge.

As she watched Grace run out the door of the house, she sank into a chair and gazed outside at the prairie. The house was quaint, but nice and clean except for the family of mice she hopefully had evicted this morning.

Her aunt came into the room and sat across from her. "How did it go?"

"Not well. It appears that the lesson plans I'd prepared are below the current skills of this child. Her grandfather taught her well."

Tonight she was going to prepare her lesson to take her to the next grade level and see how the child performed. They could always go back if this was too challenging.

But Pearl knew the girl was ready for the next level. But more than anything, she discerned the little girl was not accepting Pearl as her teacher. How could she change that and make her open to learning?

"That old man?" Edwina asked, her voice rising with speculation. "He had a good laugh when I told him about the mice. Thought you did a splendid job of catching the rodents. Chuckled at how I feared they would crawl in bed with me or get in my trunk. He may be laughing now, but he won't be for long."

Oh no! Her aunt was known for getting retribution. The two men who she'd caught cheating had received their favorite baked pie that after eating had kept them running to the outhouse. And Pearl didn't need her causing trouble.

"Aunt Edwina, you're here as their guest."

She smiled her there-will-be-retribution grin that Pearl had learned to recognize years ago meant trouble.

"Of course. But if you trap any more of our houseguests, I would like for you to save me a couple."

"Edwina," she said, warning.

Her aunt shivered. "I just want to make certain the old man experiences the same excitement we did. Don't you think that's fair?"

"His son is my employer and if you get me fired, you know Papa will use that as an excuse to require me to marry some hideous banker he's found and settle down before he gives me my trust fund."

She'd wanted to live a different life than her mother. She'd wanted to be in control of her destiny and had chosen college over marriage. And now she had to jump through another hoop in order to obtain her trust fund, then she could create her school for girls.

Why women's education wasn't as important as men's, she'd never understood, but she hoped to teach young women that they could be doctors and lawyers and mothers.

"Dear, your father is going to throw in every obstacle he can find to keep you from that money."

With a sigh, Pearl closed her eyes. "I fear you're right. But until I turn twenty-one, I will do my best to stay out of trouble and abide by his rules."

Her aunt nodded. "You know, I think I'm going to give up on love and marriage. I don't think I need it. I'm getting too old for children, and well, maybe it's time to accept I'm going to be a spinster for the rest of my days. Therefore, I'm going to live my life the way I want, and the devil take men."

Pearl opened her eyes and started laughing. "I think I heard this speech on the train after we left Chicago."

"Well, I'm just reminding myself men are off limits."

A warning bell clanged inside Pearl's head and she stared at her aunt, feeling nervous. When her aunt was the most attracted to a man, she protested she didn't like him.

Years ago, Pearl had watched her continually say she wasn't enamored of a certain man only to disappear at a party with him. So much for no interest and for staying out of trouble. Father had almost sent her to a nunnery that time.

"Which makes me think you saw someone you're intrigued by," she said, staring at her aunt.

"Who would I see? Your boss? Jesse is way too young for me though he's very handsome, but he has children and a ranch, and well, I'm just not attracted to him," her aunt said, shrugging her shoulders at her. "Though for you..."

"If I wanted to get married, I could have done that in Boston. Papa would have lined up any number of suitors. No," she said, though Jesse McIntire was a man who did make a woman's body warm at the sight of him.

She'd never experienced that breathless, hot sensation before. Never felt her blood rush, heating her from the inside out. But she didn't want to think about that. She had plans, dreams, visions of how she wanted her life and that didn't include a man.

But her aunt liked to dabble in men. Play with them like a cat, then toss them to the side. Only the man her father picked for her had married before she had a chance to send him running from the house. She'd yet to see a man her aunt couldn't handle.

"So who besides Jesse have you taken an interest in?"

"No one," she said with a smile. "Though Grandpa is a little too feisty for his own good."

"Edwina," she warned.

"Oh, good grief, the man is at least fifteen years my senior and a rascal, if ever I've met one."

Pearl shook her head and drew her brows together, feeling like the older of the two.

"Your favorite type of man," Pearl said, knowing her aunt and her penchant for trying to tame a rascal. She'd never been interested in good, wholesome men, but preferred ones she sought to change. Which often ended in her being heartbroken and disappointed when they stopped pursuing her.

"No, I've given up on men," she said again.

"For at least five minutes," Pearl responded. "Just don't get me fired."

She shrugged. "Never. But I must have something to do to keep me occupied these next few weeks before I leave for San Francisco or die of loneliness out here in this forsaken wilderness."

Pearl stared out the window at the rolling prairie, the grass swaying in the breeze, and mountains in the distance. A sense of peace came over her and she sighed. Was that how Beth had felt? Had the long, cold winter nights and the short summers, and the lack of society bored her?

Maybe, but at this moment, Pearl was enjoying the reclusiveness of the ranch. The chickens had awakened her before six and she'd risen to watch the sun rise while she drank her first cup of coffee.

The thought of getting on a train and returning to a bustling city with traffic and noise and people surrounding her, had no appeal. But she hadn't been here long and her dream of running a boarding school for young women meant she would be here for the next eight months.

"Maybe on Sunday you'll meet some ladies at church and can go into town to visit them," Pearl said, hoping that would keep her aunt busy and out of trouble.

"Maybe. Or maybe I can entertain myself by flirting with Cal."

Pearl realized she'd set her sights on the man and there was nothing that would convince her this wasn't a good idea. Nothing.

Just then Pearl heard the snap of her trap. She'd just caught another rodent.

"I think I have your mouse," she said to her aunt. Rising, she went into the kitchen where a brown mouse was trying to find a way out of the wired trap she'd created.

Her aunt was standing behind her and shuddered. "As much as I detest the animal, he'll soon be up to no good."

❧

CAL KISSED his granddaughter on the cheek. "Goodnight, pumpkin."

"Night, Grandpa," she said.

Slowly he climbed the stairs to his bed. This was the part of the evening he always hated. Even after five years, the thought of crawling into that big lonely bed with no Ida to wrap his arms around left him feeling sad.

He loved his wife and to this day, missed her. She'd been a strong woman to put up with him and his pranks. He'd loved to tease her and what had attracted him to her was how she would put him in his place.

Most women cowered when he teased or flirted with them, but his Ida had given it right back to him. The night they met, she'd told him she would never let him court her because she'd watched him flirt with women all night long. She was the only one he'd given a second dance to that night. And shown up at her daddy's house with flowers the next day.

Two months later, he'd asked her father for her hand and she'd said yes. But she never let him forget that if she caught him pollinating any flowers, he'd awaken tied to a tree with honey all over him.

For all his years with his wife, he'd taken her words to heart and never strayed. Never even wanted to stray, he'd loved that woman so much, he'd wanted to die with her when she took ill.

Opening his bedroom door, he walked inside, emptied his pockets, took off his shirt and then sat on the bed to remove his boots. After that, he stood to unbutton his pants. When he was down to his long johns, he opened the drawer in the chest and almost had a heart attack.

A little brown mouse scampered to the corner of the drawer, shivering as he gazed up at Cal in fright.

Cal laughed out loud.

So Edwina thought she could get even. She didn't know Cal McIntire. Smiling, he knew exactly what he was going to do. Grabbing his pants, he quickly donned them and then carried an old boot with the mouse out the door. The poor little fellow was a bounty. He aimed to collect.

CHAPTER 5

The next morning, Pearl opened the door to the house expecting to see Grace and her father at any moment, but instead there was a boot sitting on the porch with cheese-cloth tied around the top. A note tied to the cheesecloth.

She picked up the note and saw her aunt's name, but curiosity kept her reading.

My first mouse bounty. You owe me a kiss. Cal

"Edwina," she called.

Her aunt came to the door, drying her hands on a dishtowel. They had just finished breakfast and she'd been washing the dishes when Pearl went to set up her makeshift classroom for the day. Pearl watched her standing in the doorway a frown on her face.

"Read the note."

She leaned over and then stood up with a huff. "That old man is going to have to try harder than that to get a kiss from me. Fiddle dee dee, good luck on bringing me a rodent and thinking that's going to get him near my lips."

Pearl watched her aunt turn and walk back into the house.

Why did she fear this was going to cause her to lose her job, her trust fund, and maybe even her school? She loved her aunt dearly and respected her outrageous non-conforming ways, until it jeopardized her own dreams.

"Good morning," Jesse said as he walked up with his daughter Grace.

"Oh, sorry, I was day dreaming and staring at those mountains. I love watching the sun rising over them in the morning." It wasn't a lie. The last two mornings, she'd awaken before dawn and watched as the sun's rays bounced on the peaks turning them the most beautiful shades of purple and gold.

He smiled and then pushed Grace toward her. "One day I'll take you riding in the mountains. You'll enjoy the scenery even more."

Grace glanced up at her father. "I want to go."

"Of course," he said gazing at his daughter. "You can show her the wild huckleberry bushes."

"We pick the berries before the bears get to them and make jam and even a pie. They're really good, but the bears love them," Grace said.

The thought of bears eating in the same location as where picking berries sent a little shiver through Pearl. She liked adventure, but definitely on the safe side.

"I'd love to go berry picking with you when they're in season."

The little girl smiled. "What are we going to learn today? I'd rather go riding with Pa today. Maybe we could learn tomorrow."

The way the child said the words, it was like she was negotiating with Pearl. And that wasn't going to happen.

"But class is every day," Pearl said softly.

Her father patted her on the back. "Saturday. We'll go riding and fishing on Saturday." He glanced at Pearl, his dark earthy eyes making her feel warm. "You're welcome to join us."

"I'd like to go," Pearl said, glancing at the man and his daughter. Her heart swelled and she pushed the thoughts racing through her out of her mind. He was her dead cousin's man. Why was she so physically attracted?

It would never do, and she didn't have time for a man in her life. She had things she wanted to do that didn't include a Colorado rancher. "We better get started. Yesterday, Grace was far more advanced than I'd counted on. Today, I'm going to try to challenge her a little more."

Jesse smiled and hugged his daughter. "Study hard."

She looked at her father and shook her head. "I'd rather go riding."

"I know, but you're going to study."

The girl didn't answer, but rather stomped up the wooden steps that led into the house. She disappeared inside without saying goodbye.

Jesse shook his head as he watched his daughter vanish into the house. "Let me know if she gives you any trouble."

"We'll be fine," Pearl said not feeling certain, but wanting to appear she could handle the situation. And she could. She wasn't about to let a seven-year-old best her.

"Have a good day," Jesse said, touching the brim of his large cowboy hat.

Pearl watched him walk away, his chaps swishing as he strode toward the barn. Why now, did her body notice a man. She'd gone through three years of college and never been attracted to her schoolmates, and yet the moment she'd seen Jesse, it was like the sight had her lungs shrinking and her heart pounding like it was in a race.

And the sight of his full lips, blue eyes, and strong cheekbones left her wanting to run her finger along his stubborn chin. Maybe it was the ruggedness of the man. He wasn't one of those stiff-necked bankers her father had paraded in front of her. No, Jesse McIntire was like a breath of Colorado mountain air to this girl from Boston.

ॐ

AFTER GRACE and Pearl went into the house, Edwina took her needlework and sat outside on the porch. She was just waiting for Cal to come by and she was going to let him know he'd be waiting until he had frostbite before she would accept his kiss.

Just then Cal came out of the barn, pulling two saddled horses by their reins. As he walked, she couldn't help but notice the ruggedness about the rancher. And yet when he stopped in front and gazed at her from beneath his hat, she could see the twinkle in his emerald eyes. The man was mischief with a capital M and for some reason that intrigued her.

"Good morning, ma'am," he said, grinning at her, baiting her to respond to his message, but she wasn't going to. She refused. "I trust you slept well?"

"Excellent, how about yourself? Nothing creepy, crawly kept you awake last night?"

He laughed. "No, in fact, I left the little bugger in a boot on the porch for you. Did you see my note?"

The man was handsome with only a smudge of gray at his temples, and the way he wore that cowboy hat pulled down low over his forehead, his full lips turned up in that cocky grin, made her eyes lock on him. He was not about to get the better of her. Many a man had tried and they no longer had her acquaintance.

"My niece found it and asked me what was going on? I told her just a man's wish and a prayer."

He winked at her. "But it's a good wish. You can't blame a man for trying."

"Dreaming is more like it," she responded, her heart hammering in her chest. The man was cocky and handsome and way too assuming.

Still there was nothing like a frisky man chasing after a woman and she'd let Cal pursue her, but he would never catch her. After her last disastrous engagement, maybe the time had come to give up on ever finding a companion who was interesting and cared about her.

Her brother had funneled men her way for years and all of them bored her, even the last one she had become engaged to out of sheer desperation. But no more.

The thought of living a nomadic life, moving from town to town, letting men vie for her attention sounded like more fun than returning to Boston and the ever-watchful eye of her brother. A shudder rippled through her. She wanted an interesting man in her life. One who kept her laughing and on her toes.

"I thought maybe you'd like to go riding with me this morning," he said, that twinkle back in his eyes. The one that both attracted and warned her away. Yet the thought of spending time alone with the man was both intriguing and risky.

"I see you've already saddled the horses. I think you're being a little presumptuous to assume I would go with you. After all, you probably think you would receive a kiss while we were gone."

The man had nerve to assume she'd go riding with him. Though part of her thought it sounded like a splendid idea.

He shook his head. "Oh no, ma'am. I learned long ago never to assume anything about a woman. This horse is for my son. I'd have to go back and saddle the old nag for you."

She gasped. "Did you just call me an old nag?"

"Never, ma'am. But I wouldn't want you to ride one of our spirited work horses. I'd insist on you riding Old Nag. That's her name."

"You had the audacity to name your horse Old Nag?"

Laughing, he pushed his hat back. The urge to run her fingers along his cheekbones overcame her, but there was enough distance between them that she didn't have to worry. "My wife named the horse, not me."

That was unusual. "Why would she name the horse an old nag?"

"Because the mare was old when I bought her, and my wife said I'd been taken. She didn't think the horse would be around long. The old girl has been with us going on ten years."

Edwina couldn't help but admire his wife for calling him out and naming a horse that he'd bought. Yet the animal had outlived both of their expectations.

"Wow, I guess she wasn't as old as you thought she was."

"No, ma'am. She's a good horse and she's gentle. I wouldn't want to risk you getting hurt and you could still ride a side saddle if you chose."

Edwina bit her lip as she stared at the muscled trim of Cal. For a man over a decade her senior, he was quite handsome. She'd like nothing better than to go riding with him but would that send the wrong signal?

She didn't want to be available, but she wanted to get out and see the countryside. She stared down at the needlework in her hands. She was sick to death of doing something genteel and ladylike. She wanted to step out of her comfort zone, out of her boundaries.

"I promise, we won't go far. And when you're ready we'll come back."

Part of her wanted to tell him no, but another part thought it would be wonderful to get out of the house. It'd been years since she'd ridden. She could continue to sit here on this porch, looking out, never experiencing life or she could go riding with this very challenging man.

She sighed. No, she was done with men. As much as she hated needlework, she was going to find some way to occupy her time that didn't include a devilishly rakish man that intrigued her.

"Thanks for the invite, but I think I'll pass."

He glanced at her and smiled. "I know you want to go."

She gave him her disapproving frown but didn't disavow what he said. "Good day, Cal."

He grinned. "I'm not giving up. You will go riding with me and soon."

Tipping his hat at her, he turned and walked away, pulling the horses behind him.

He was a tempting man. But her luck with men was less than good. And maybe it was time to take a break.

∮⋆

LATER THAT EVENING, Pearl stepped out on the porch of the house and stared up at the stars twinkling in the night sky. As much as she liked living in Boston, this was peaceful, serene and quiet.

Gazing into the yard, she heard the lonely moo of a cow and breathed in the cool crisp air. With a shiver, she wrapped her shawl tighter around her shoulders, grateful she'd slipped it on before stepping outside.

They'd had dinner tonight at the main house. Cal and Grace were there, but Jesse had been missing. He'd been delayed in the field, and after they'd eaten, she'd returned to their little sanctuary to glance through her books to find something that would interest Grace.

She didn't want to spend her time learning. And today she'd oozed resentment at having to stay inside while her father rode the range.

"Good evening," the deep voice said, walking out of the darkness into the light.

"Good evening," Pearl replied, her voice coming out in a swoosh as warmth flooded her at the sound of Jesse. The man's deep tenor had a way of radiating excitement through her body. She just needed to ignore the feelings.

He walked up the steps of the house and sank down into one

of the rockers on the porch. "I would continue standing, but I'm bushed."

"That's fine," she said, leaning back against the porch railing. "You weren't at supper, tonight."

For some reason she'd missed seeing him sitting at the end of the table, next to his daughter. While the four of them ate, it felt like they're had been a missing piece.

"No, it took longer than I expected today. We have more calves this year and sorting out which ones we want to sell and which ones to keep is always challenging," he said, removing his hat and laying it on his leg. "I was worried after I left you today that Grace might have given you trouble. She has a stubborn streak."

No doubt. But what could Pearl say? If she told him the truth, then he'd say something to Grace which would only cause more resentment. She'd rather try to deal with the child her way and hope that soon the child would look forward to her lessons each day. But for now, she had to get past this wall of animosity.

"She was fine. It's going to take time before she accepts that I'm here to help her."

How much time, Pearl had no idea, but the child was being stubborn and didn't want to participate when Pearl tried to talk to her about different subjects. They'd briefly touched on geography and the girl had almost gone to sleep, she'd been so bored.

He nodded. "I understand, but I don't want her to waste your time. While you're here, I want my daughter to learn."

She shrugged. "It's only been two days. I'll give you updates, but already I know she's a smart little girl who is ahead of her age group. She's reading on a third grade level. It's going to take time for the two of us to learn each other's strength,s and by the time I leave, she'll be ready for either boarding school or another teacher."

"Boarding school?" he said, his voice raising, his body stiffening.

Startled at his strong reaction, Pearl leaned against the pillar. "What's wrong with boarding school."

"I'm not sending my daughter off to someplace where I don't know if she'll be well taken care of and I can't get to her quickly if she needed me."

Pearl shrugged. "Then she'll need another teacher to help you finish educating her. As I will be leaving in January."

She was only planning on being here until she felt] she could return home. She knew her father had said February, but she'd go back sooner if she could.

Jesse gave a little snort. "I hate to tell you this, but no one gets out of here in January. By then, the snow is piled high and if the train runs, it's a miracle. I would plan on staying until at least March. Even then it will be questionable if you're going to be able to get out of town."

She frowned. "You can't have more snow than we have in Boston."

Boston had enough snow sometimes to shut down the town, but not for months at a time.

"Yes, we do," he said with a laugh.

Could her father have known she would not be able to leave in January like she'd planned. Her birthday was in February and she had every intention of starting her boarding school in time for the fall session. She couldn't return earlier than January because she'd promised she would stay until then.

She sighed. "I need to be back in Boston no later than February. But then again, maybe my father knew by sending me here, I couldn't return in the winter."

He frowned. "What is so important that you return by February?"

She had no idea how much he knew about her situation and she wasn't certain as to tell him or not, but then decided what could it hurt? Only if he was working with her father, and somehow she didn't get that feeling.

"On my twenty-first birthday, I receive my trust fund."

He shrugged and stared at her. "All right, why can't you wait to receive your trust fund."

"My father is in charge of it and if I'm not at the lawyer's office, then they can reinvest the money. I must be present to claim I want the funds according to my father."

Jesse's forehead wrinkled like he was deep in thought and then he turned up those luscious eyes on her that had her heart skipping a beat. What was it about this man that awakened parts of her body in ways she'd never felt before?

She knew he didn't want her here. He'd made that clear the night they spoke in his office, yet she felt drawn to him.

"Miss Weare, I would suggest you contact the trust manager and verify this information. I've never heard of someone having to be there in person. I'm not saying I'm right but write to him and ask him what are the terms to receive your trust fund."

Why hadn't she thought to do that before? With everything else, why should she take her father's word. She would write the manager tonight. Maybe they could take her letter into town with them on Sunday and she could drop it in the post box.

"Thank you," she said. "I never considered that my father might conceal the correct details, but that makes sense. He's tried to stop me before."

His brows drew together. "What is it you plan on doing with your trust fund?"

She'd told other men before and none of them had appreciated her dreams. They'd made fun of her.

"I'm going to build my own boarding school where young women can be educated like men."

Jesse McIntire didn't laugh, but he obviously didn't approve either.

"No wonder your father is trying to stop you from wasting your money."

"Why would it be a waste to educate young women? You have a daughter, don't you want her to be as smart as any man?"

"Of course. And I have no problem with women being educated," he said, standing from the chair and putting his hat on his head. "It's just that the world is not ready to accept that a woman, even if she is smarter than a man, can be educated and learn a profession."

It was true, society had yet to accept that a woman could be as educated as a man. But hopefully sometime in the near future that would change, and women would even be allowed to vote.

"Is that why you don't want to send Grace to a boarding school? You don't think she needs to learn?"

He walked up within inches of Pearl and she inhaled the sharp scent of the man, sending her pulse racing through her. "I love my daughter. I'm responsible for her upbringing. Sending her off to a fancy school is putting that responsibility into someone else's hands."

He took a deep breath and released it slowly. "By the time she's grown, she will be educated, and know how to run a ranch. Grace will be a strong woman who can take care of herself. Unlike her mother who attended a fancy boarding school and didn't know diddly and depended on the servants to care for her. That's not happening to my daughter."

He was much too close to her, and for a moment, she feared he was going to kiss her as he licked his lips and gazed into her eyes. Her heart pounded in her chest as she waited, wanting to feel his lips against her own. Then he touched the tip of his hat and took a step back. "Goodnight, Miss Weare."

When Pearl walked into the house, her heart was hammering in her chest. There was something about Jesse McIntire and she needed to keep him at a distance. No more late night talks on her porch.

At this time in her life, she didn't have any plans on a becoming involved with a man, most especially the man whose daughter she was teaching. She had dreams and those dreams didn't include a handsome rancher with a seven-year-old daughter.

Quickly, she undressed and slipped into her nightgown. Crawling into bed, she reached over and turned off the lamp. A snapping sound came from the kitchen and she knew her mouse cage had just caught another rodent. How many more could there be?

The flame of the lantern slowly died, and she lay in bed thinking about her life, wondering if she was making the right decision regarding her school. She'd joined the women's movement in order not to become like her mother, an intelligent woman smothered by societal rules, unable to do anything without her husband's permission.

Pearl refused to live that kind of life. Her mother had died an angry, embittered woman who'd been too smart for her own good. Pearl answered to no man except her father and she was desperately trying to separate her life from his.

Releasing a deep breath, she settled in to sleep and that's when she felt something slimy move against her leg. With a cry, she jumped out of bed, her imagination filled with images of snakes. Quickly, she struck a match to the light.

Picking up the lantern, she shined the light on her bedsheets, knowing it would be hard to sleep tonight. Two green frogs gazed up at her, all innocent eyed. A shudder rippled down her spine and she knew exactly what she would do.

Grace McIntire was sending her a message, but Pearl was just as stubborn. She needed this job until she could strike out on her own. And Grace needed a woman's touch.

CHAPTER 6

*P*earl's skirts billowed out over the back of the horse, but she rode the animal with practiced ease. Even in Boston, a young woman was taught how to ride. And Pearl had learned at an early age how a proper lady rode a horse.

But she longed to make one of those skirts where a woman could ride a horse like a man. Where she didn't sit precariously on the edge of a saddle fearful of the horse galloping off and bouncing her right out of her perch.

She glanced at the two riders ahead of her. Jesse sat on a horse like he'd been born in the saddle. He rode with the grace and agility of a man who made his living riding the range.

His daughter sat in the saddle like a boy in her pants, her hair pulled back out of her face, a hat perched on her head. Grace would be a beauty if she ever matured and decided to dress like a girl.

A breeze blew out of the mountains, stirring the leaves on the trees, whispering a lonesome sound. They'd been riding alongside a creek now for quite a while and Pearl guessed they must have a perfect spot they liked to fish.

The Boreal Chorus Frog - Pseudacris maculata, according to

her science textbook, were inside her saddle bags, ready to be released back into the wild. But first a science lesson.

They pulled their horses to a halt and Grace jumped off her mare and ran to the river. For a moment, Pearl's heart almost stopped beating as she watched the little girl lean over the rushing water tumbling over rocks, gurgling to some unknown destination. But her father didn't seem to do anything to stop her.

Jesse came over and put his warm hands on Pearl's waist as he lifted her off the side saddle. A tingle of awareness zinged through her as she breathed in his clean manly scent. She gazed into his earthy eyes and licked her lips. When her feet landed on the ground, she released the breath she'd been holding.

Why did her body seem to thrum like a guitar when he was around? Why did her blood warm, rushing through her like the babbling river and why when she looked at him did she imagine the feel of his lips on hers?

"Have you ever been fishing before?" he asked her, stepping away.

"No," she said, "this is my first time."

He leaned in closer. "Let Grace show you how. It might help her to bond with you."

She nodded. "But first, I want to show Grace something."

"All right," he said, moving as she reached into her saddle bags.

A shudder ripped through her when her hands touched the first frog. They were creepy animals, but they ate bugs. "Grace."

"Yes, Miss Weare?" she said, running up to the two of them, her blond hair bouncing on her shoulders.

"I thought today you could be the teacher and show me how to fish. I've never been before, and your dad was telling me how excellent you are at catching trout."

The little girl's eyes grew large and she smiled. "Come on, let's get started. We need to find a perfect spot."

Pearl had no idea about fishing, but before Grace taught her, she wanted to rid herself of the frogs.

"But first, I have two frogs that somehow managed to get in the house. I thought here, close to the stream, would be a good place to let them go. Come, look at them, Grace."

Jesse was busy unloading the fishing gear from the back of his horse. Grace glanced over at her father and then back at Pearl as if she were unsure as to her motives. "Where did you find those frogs?"

"In my bed." Pearl knelt to her eye level holding the animals who were flailing their legs trying to get away. She would not give the child the satisfaction of knowing how much they had scared her that night. Instead, she would use this as a teaching moment.

"Notice the darker stripes down his brownish red back. That one strip goes right through his eye and down the side of his body. Look at his back legs, they're shorter than the front ones to give him more strength when he leaps. Now help me find him and his brother a nice boggy area that has rocks for them to bed down in."

Grace gazed at her, her eyes wide and knowing, and Pearl knew she'd placed the animals in her bed. "Won't they get cold?"

"Oh no, they hibernate. They'll be just fine."

Frankly, as long as they were out of the house and her bed, she really didn't care about the welfare of the frogs, but she also knew from what she'd read about them that they did hibernate.

The child raised her brows and then ran over to the creek. "We don't want them close to where we'll be fishing," she called out as she ran along the banks of the river, giving Pearl's heart a jolt as she teetered on the edge. The water wasn't deep but was moving swiftly and she knew it would be cold. If the child fell in, how far downstream would she be swept before they could pull her out?

Carrying both frogs in her hands, she hurried to catch up with Grace.

"I think I found the perfect place," she said.

Pearl reached her and looked around the muddy area, the rocks, and even some dead twigs were close to the water. "I think this is perfect. Now here, you take this one and let him go. And I'll release his brother."

"How do you know they're brothers? What if they're sisters?"

A chuckle escaped from Pearl. "You're absolutely right. They could be sisters. Okay, on the count of three, let yours go and then I'll release mine."

Pearl counted and the child released the frog. Pearl let hers go. The two frogs didn't move for a moment and then they both jumped into the water swimming for their freedom.

Grace looked at Pearl, her gaze accusatory. "Those were my favorite frogs."

The child was learning a consequence to her actions, but Pearl wasn't sure she understood.

Pearl shrugged. "If you wanted to keep them, all you had to do was explain to your father how they were put in my bed."

A frown appeared between Grace's eyes and somehow Pearl didn't think that could be good. "Let's go back and get our fishing poles and you can show me how to fish."

The girl jumped up from where she'd been squatted. "Let's go."

Pearl began to walk back toward Jesse, the creek running alongside her, the water tumbling over rocks.

Grace walked beside her. She glanced at Pearl and smiled. "You're going to love fishing. But first you have to put a squishy worm on your hook for the trout to eat. You get worm guts on your fingers."

"I know how to wash my hands in the creek." If she thought that a little worm juice would scare Pearl off, she was mistaken.

The girl frowned.

"Oh, look, Pa's already got the poles set up," she bumped Pearl and then took off running.

Just that little nudge was enough to knock Pearl's balance off. Her feet slid on the muddy embankment and she felt herself falling toward the river. She tried to regain her balance, but she landed with a splash in the rushing water on her backside.

Cold seeped through her skirts, causing her to shiver. The current tugged at her and she felt herself sliding and knew that if she was dragged out into the main part of the river, she could very easily be hurt by the water rushing over the rocks.

She dug her boots into the soft bottom, fighting the pull of the water. But they weren't holding. Slowly her skirts were being yanked by the current toward the middle of the creek.

Suddenly Jesse splashed into the water, pulling her out. The feel of his strong arms around her upper arms was reassuring. When they reached the bank, he pulled her to her feet. "Grace, get a blanket out of the saddle bags."

Pearl stood in shock, shaking with fright. He wrapped his arms around her and held her. "You okay?"

"I think so," she said, her heart pounding in her chest, her knees quaking, her skirts sodden and cold. "The water was pulling me. I don't think I would have lasted much longer."

Jesse held her in his arms and patted her on the back. "It was the weight of your skirts. With them water-logged, there was no way you could have fought the current."

She leaned her forehead against his shoulder, enjoying the feel of his strong arms around her, the feel of his heart pounding against hers, the warmth of his body. "Thank you. If you hadn't pulled me out, I hate to think what would have happened."

"I would have thrown you a rope and pulled you out," he said. "I wouldn't have let anything bad happen to you," he whispered softly in her ear and squeezed her.

A shiver of warmth radiated from her core surprising her.

She'd never experienced that feeling before. She stepped out of his arms. "Look at me. I'm getting you all wet."

The look in his eyes was lighting a bonfire within her. She licked her lips knowing that if Grace hadn't been there, she would have done more than just wrapped her arms around him.

"I brought you a blanket," Grace said, interrupting. She gazed between the two of them, her eyes narrowed. "But now you've got Pa wet. I'll go get him one too."

She ran back to the horses and Jesse watched his daughter leave. "We need to get you out of those wet clothes. I'll build a fire and then you can strip down to your petticoats."

Laughter bubbled up within her. He thought she was going to strip down to her pantaloons in front of him and his daughter. Her reputation would never recover if anyone ever learned that she'd paraded around in her under clothing in front of a man and his daughter.

"Mr. McIntire, there is no way I am going to remove my dress in front of you and Grace."

"Miss Weare, oh, good grief," he exclaimed as he ran his hand through his hair. "Can I please call you Pearl? I think it's time we dropped this pretense and accepted that you'll be here awhile."

She could tell he wanted to say more but held back. What would he have said? It was like they were circling each other, waiting for the first one to make a move, when Grace wasn't around.

She gave him her haughtiest smile. "Yes, you may call me Pearl, but I'm not removing my skirt in front of your daughter."

He sighed. "Look, I have an extra set of pants I carry with me. You can wear those while we're fishing. I'll build a fire and while your skirt and petticoats dry, you can wear my pants.

"I'll keep my back turned until you tell me it's okay, but you can't stay in that wet clothing and it would take us an hour to return to the ranch."

Already, Pearl's teeth were chattering with cold and she tried to hide her shivering from him, knowing he would really object if he knew just how frigid she was and how her toes were almost numb from the ice water in that creek.

She didn't want to ruin the outing for them, but if they left now, she'd be frozen by the time they returned to the ranch. Even in the summertime, that water was nothing but melting snow. But when a body was wet, one could easily catch a cold or pneumonia.

"All right. You build a fire to dry my skirt and petticoats and I'll wear your pants and shirt."

She wondered about the feel and smell of his clothing on her body. And would this be appropriate in front of a young child that had very little respect for rules? But if she objected, then she'd ruin their outing and Grace would have more reason to hate her.

He smiled. "Thank you. I just didn't want you to catch a cold. And well, Grace has been looking forward to fishing."

Grace ran up and shoved a blanket at Jesse. "Here, Pa. You're wet too."

"Thank you, but I'm not near as wet as Miss Weare."

The little girl gave her a peevish look. Pearl was almost certain she'd deliberately pushed her into the river, but she wouldn't let the child win.

Jesse had called her Miss Weare in front of Grace instead of using her given name. She really should object to him calling her Pearl, but she liked the sound of her name on his lips. She liked the fact that he was worried about her. And she liked the fact he was trying to make everyone happy.

"Let's get you those clothes," Jesse said and the three of them walked toward the horses.

CHAPTER 7

*W*hen he first heard the splash, he'd immediately feared Grace had finally gotten too close to the edge of the river and fallen in. He'd warned her repeatedly, but the child never paid much heed to his warnings.

His heart stopped and he'd turned and started running toward the sound. Then, he'd seen his daughter and knew Pearl had fallen in. Grace was skipping toward him, and she pointed to the spot where Pearl had gone in.

He reached her just as the river buoyed up her skirt enough that she was beginning to lose ground against the current. Though the river wasn't really deep, the melting snow in the higher elevations had it moving at a fast clip.

The rushing water could have picked her up and carried her downstream, smashing her against the rocks and boulders. What if he hadn't reached her? What if she'd gotten hurt?

The woman continued to surprise him. When he'd stood her up, she'd been shaking, but she hadn't cried. Hadn't demanded to go back to the ranch. Hadn't even whimpered. If that had been Beth, she would have carried on so loudly, she'd have run off any wildlife within miles.

Once, she'd fallen in the snow and when he picked her up, she'd almost hit him. As if it were his fault she'd lost her footing.

Pearl couldn't hide the fear he'd seen in her beautiful brown eyes, but she'd pulled herself together and only gave him a small amount of trouble with regards to taking off her wet clothes and putting on his pants.

"Grace, stand back away from the river," he called. He didn't need to rescue another one of them this afternoon.

Pearl had suffered enough for one day, though she didn't realize that the hem of her skirt had been floating almost to her knees in the water and had given him a brief glance of her pantaloons.

Now she stood next to his daughter away from the edge of the river. Their two heads were bent close talking as Grace showed her how to catch trout in the pools close to the bank.

His pants were big on her but covered her decently and left him imaging what the rest of her looked like now that he'd seen up to her knees. He'd like nothing more than to catch a glimpse of her curves.

And holding her close, he couldn't help but notice the sweet scent of lavender and roses on her. Now his pants and shirt would hold her scent and that was strangely enticing.

"Pa, we caught one," Grace cried, running toward him, her fish dangling from the pole.

"Put it in the basket," he said.

He refused to coddle his daughter and he watched her expertly remove the hook from the trout's mouth and put the fish in the basket. "We're ahead."

"Yes, you are," he said, gazing at Pearl who stood next to Grace.

If his daughter hadn't been here today, it could have gotten very interesting with her in his arms. He'd forgotten how it felt to hold a woman, to comfort her. The scent of lavender with just a hint of desire that had him remembering how he'd enjoyed being with Beth until they'd returned to Colorado.

Glancing at Pearl, he realized...she wouldn't be here long. Today only proved she was out of place in Colorado. The sooner she left to return to Boston, the better. She reminded him of everything he'd loved about his wife. He couldn't forget the way Beth hadn't belonged here, just as Pearl would never like being here.

CHAPTER 8

The next morning as they all filled a pew in church, Pearl said a little prayer of thanksgiving for being rescued from the river, but she also asked for guidance on how to handle Grace.

She was certain the girl had pushed her into the river yesterday. While she didn't believe the child had meant to harm her, she wondered at the lengths she would go to keep from learning.

She'd also noticed how Grace was watching her father and Pearl. Could the child feel this draw that Pearl felt toward Jesse?

Good grief, if she thought Pearl was pursuing her father, she would come after her with a vengeance. As she clearly did not like to share Jesse with anyone.

As they sang the last hymn, Pearl couldn't help but glance around the little church at the members. They'd all been so inviting, so welcoming, that she'd felt at peace here.

Then she would remember why she was in Russell Gulch. If any of them knew that she'd been arrested and thrown in jail for protesting the right to vote, how they would feel?

Once she had her school going, she would once again be

involved with helping women have the same rights as men. In the meantime, she tried to keep her suffragette ambitions to herself like her aunt suggested. But it was hard.

When the service ended, the reverend was waiting for them at the door. "I'm Mr. Garrison. I'm only here about once a month or for special occasions. So glad you came. And how are you related to Jesse and Cal?"

"I'm not. I'm his wife Beth's cousin. I came to teach Grace. And this is my aunt Edwina Weare," Pearl said, noticing the man's wife hurrying toward them.

"Hello, ladies," she said. "I'm Mrs. Garrison. It's so nice to meet you and to know that sweet child is being taught."

Pearl watched as Grace slipped away, running off to join other children, her pigtails flying behind her, her shirt and pants clinging to her little girl body. Pearl had tried to talk her into a dress, but she refused.

"We're glad you're here. Grace is quite the rambunctious child," the reverend said to Pearl. Jesse had slipped away and was talking to some men who were huddled together.

"I'll only be here until January," she said and watched the reverend's eyes widen. "I know Mr. McIntire has been telling me it's awfully hard to get out of Colorado in the dead of winter."

"Last winter was our worst winter in twenty years. Most of the cattlemen lost a lot of their herd. It was a tough year," Mrs. Garrison said. "The train doesn't run as often in the wintertime."

"I'll keep that in mind," Pearl said.

Pearl glanced out and saw a group of children and one of the girls was poking a stick at Grace, tugging at her shirt. The children all laughed, and Grace stomped away. Another little girl ran after Grace and put her arm around her. Something was going on and Pearl needed to know.

"Excuse me, Reverend. Great sermon by the way, but I need to check on Grace. I'll see you next month."

She tried to slip up behind Grace and listen to the conversation.

"Don't cry, Grace. You know how mean she is. I wish I could wear pants and a shirt."

"My Pa likes me to wear what I have on," Grace said.

"My Pa is getting married again. I'm getting a new momma," her friend confided.

"Did you want a new momma," Grace asked.

The little girl shrugged. "As long as she's nice to me, it would be okay. You've got those two ladies living at your house. I bet you're going to get a new momma soon."

Oh geez, just what she didn't need. Some little girl filling Grace's head about her becoming her mother. If Grace even thought for a moment that was possibly true, she would give Pearl fits. She had to somehow let her know this wasn't happening.

"Excuse me, miss." A red headed boy interrupted her eaves-dropping.

"Yes," she asked, wondering what this boy would want with her.

"Are you that new teacher out at the McIntire Ranch?"

"Yes, I'm Miss Weare," she said, gazing at the beautiful boy who had the softest looking skin she'd ever seen on a young man.

"I'm Lance Baker," he said, reaching out and shaking her hand. "I like to read. It's kind of a hobby of mine and I was wondering if I came out to the ranch, if you'd let me borrow some of your books?"

Pearl glanced at the young man. There was something odd, but yet compelling about him. She wanted to help the boy. "Of course. I have a trunk and brought a lot of books with me. Come by and choose one. Once you're finished with that one, you can return it and get another one."

The boy's face lit with excitement. "Thank you. I'll be by later today."

Pearl smiled at his enthusiasm. Why couldn't her pupil be more like that and want to learn. "I look forward to seeing you."

He ran off and Grace turned, giving her another of her accusatory glares. The child knew she'd been eavesdropping. "Sorry, I was coming to get you. Your father is ready to leave."

Grace frowned. "Bye, Mary. See you next time."

Mary glanced at Pearl, her eyes gazing at her and then she turned back to Grace. "She's pretty." Leaning in she whispered, "She'd make you a good momma."

Oh dear, this child was not making things easier for Pearl. "Let's go, Grace. They're waiting on us."

CHAPTER 9

On the ride home from church, Pearl was placed beside Jesse in the wagon. She sat next to him, watching his hands handle the reins, occasionally bumping against him as they traveled the road back to the ranch, making him feel uncomfortable.

Since the fishing trip, there had been this knowing acknowledgement between them. Sitting beside her was difficult as she brushed up against him. Part of him was enjoying the feel of her woman's body way too much with his daughter sitting not far away.

"How did you like our little church?" he asked, glancing at her before his eyes returned to the road. The people in the small community had welcomed Pearl and her aunt.

"It's a nice church," she said. "The people were friendly and the message was a good one."

"What's your church like in Boston?" he asked to be friendly, not really caring, but enjoying talking to Pearl. He liked that she had different viewpoints than most women he'd met. Beth had been dependent on him, but Pearl was fighting for her independence. It was intriguing.

"It's very large. My family has attended that same church for at least three generations."

"So everyone knows you."

"I wouldn't say that," she said. "This was such a nice change."

His family had been some of the first settlers in Russell Gulch, living outside of town before Michael Russell discovered gold. But the mine had turned a spot in the road into a village and maybe someday a city.

"Glad you enjoyed it. Do you miss Boston?" he asked wondering where that question had come from. He hadn't expected to ask her, in fact, he didn't care. She would be returning soon, and this tempting woman would be gone, leaving him alone once again.

"I miss my friends from school, but there's nothing back there. My mother passed away years ago, my father would like to marry me off, and my stepmother is probably dancing now that I'm gone. I'm playing father's game until I can obtain my inheritance. Then I'll decide where to build my school."

"Why do you want to build a girl's school? Why not just teach and let someone else handle the administration," he questioned thinking it would be so much easier than dealing with the legalities and the parents. Not to mention creating an institution from the ground up would be costly and time-consuming. What drove a woman to start her own business?

"I want to be in charge of my own destiny. I don't want to answer to anyone, especially a headmistress of a private institution."

A frown furrowed his forehead. "What's wrong with working for someone?"

"Everything. I don't want to be told what I have to or can teach. I want to show my students everything, not just what the school thinks they should know."

What was it that Miss Weare wanted to teach that she knew

a school would disapprove of? What was she teaching his daughter?

"What exactly do you want to teach that you fear other people would find objectionable?"

Grace leaned forward and tapped her father on the back. "Pa, can I go to Mary's birthday party next week? Did you hear she's getting a new mother? Her pa is getting married. I'm so glad that you aren't ever getting married again. I don't want a new mother."

Pearl smiled at Jesse. "Things like the women's right to vote. Have a bank account and be in charge of her destiny. I'm a suffragette."

Stunned, he continued driving, thinking about what Pearl had just told him. He'd figured she'd come to Colorado because of some scandal, but he'd never considered her to be one of those women he'd heard of fighting for their rights.

"I'm a little shocked."

To get her father's attention, the girl almost climbed over the seat.

"Grace, we'll talk about Mary's birthday party later. For now, you need to sit back and let me get us home."

Jesse retreated. He didn't know what to say, the first woman he was attracted to since his wife died was a suffragette. One of those women fighting for the right to vote and to do anything else that a man could do.

It wasn't that he was against women voting. He just didn't understand what they thought they were missing out on. All his life, he'd treated women like they were to be protected and honored and cherished. What more could they want? What more had Beth wanted that he'd been unable to give her?

THE NEXT MORNING, Edwina was sitting outside sipping a delicious cup of hot tea while Pearl was inside teaching her pupil. The little girl was sweet and precocious and was not enjoying being forced to learn with Pearl.

When her niece walked in Saturday afternoon looking like she'd gotten into a cat fight with a river rat and the rat had won, Edwina had wanted to march up the hill to the big house and let that child know a new sheriff was in town and she wouldn't be getting away with meanness any longer.

It had taken Pearl a few minutes to talk some sense into her and to let her handle the situation. But the child was walking a fine line and if something happened to her niece, she'd be all over her like a bear on honey.

A cool breeze blew a tendril of hair across Edwina's cheek as she gazed out at the busy ranch, waiting. Yesterday, that fool man Cal had tried to hold her hand during church. And then on the way back, he winked at her.

He was being a rapscallion with his teasing and flirting and she was playing him. At this point in her life, she was questioning her need for a man. Why couldn't she just enjoy them, but not marry one. Why not flirt, tease, and then move on? Men did it, why couldn't women.

And then she saw him walking out of the barn toward her. There was a quickness in his step that somehow had her heart pumping a little harder. For a man in his early fifties, there was a jauntiness about him that had her catching her breath.

"Good morning, Edwina," he said walking up to the first step of the porch. "Are you going riding with me this morning?" He paused gazing at her. "You've turned me down four times now. If I wasn't a patient man, I wouldn't ask again."

"All right, Cal, I'll go riding with you."

A big grin crossed his face. "You wait right here while I get the horses."

Edwina laughed as she watched him almost running to the barn. Fifteen minutes later, he was back with the two horses.

"Is this the Old Nag?"

"She's a good horse. One that I trust not to pitch you off."

Edwina laid her needlework down and walked down the steps. She stepped into the stirrup and Cal helped her settle into the side saddle. "Lord, I don't know why I agreed to this."

"Because I am a handsome man that you wanted to spend the morning seeing the countryside with."

She shook her head at him. "Yes, I know I'm crazy."

He grinned over at her. "But isn't crazy fun?"

She made a clicking noise and nudged the horse. The old nag began to walk. "Are you coming?"

"I'm right behind you," he responded. "We're going to ride along the ridge of those hills in the distance. There's a really nice path that makes a circle and comes back to the ranch."

"This isn't going to take all day is it?" she asked, not wanting to be gone too long, but enjoying his company.

"Oh no, we'll be back in time for lunch."

He trotted his horse up beside her and she glanced at him. The man was beauty and perfection riding the animal and his body moved in time with the gait. She felt a quickening in her breath when she gazed at him and wondered why this man. But she was having more fun with him than she ever had, and she had no serious intentions regarding him.

Thirty minutes later, they reached the top of the hill and he pulled his horse to a stop. For a moment, they sat silently looking out over the ranch, gazing at the beautiful property.

"You built this with your wife?" she asked.

"Yes, we moved here right after we were married and lived here almost thirty years before she passed away. I can't imagine living anywhere else. Don't have any desire to even see the big city."

Shaking her head, she looked at him. "You're not missing

anything there. This is absolutely gorgeous. I can't get over how clean and crisp the air is here compared to Boston."

"No factories," he responded. "We have mines in the area, but that's all."

"Let's rest a few minutes here," he said climbing from his horse.

He came over to her and lifted her from the side saddle. They stood, gazing into each other's eyes. Her chest felt like she couldn't get enough air as she wanted to reach out and touch him, but resisted her body's demands. Finally, she said, "And what were you doing in church yesterday?"

Though he'd done it discreetly where no one could see, she'd felt his hand reach out and squeeze hers during the sermon.

He grinned. "Trying to hold your hand. What better place than in church."

She laughed. "Cal McIntire, what are you doing? You're playing with fire and I've been known to burn men."

"Well, honey, let's just hope you light the match in the right place at the right time."

The man was outrageous and yet she couldn't help but like him.

Her mouth opened and she stared. "I don't know whether to laugh or be insulted."

"I think you should be honored that you're the first woman I've had a serious interest in since my wife died."

"Serious?"

What was he talking about? She was determined not to become involved with men again, yet there was something about Cal that was fun, that was intriguing, and she felt the need for just a little more of the man.

"Well, you know. One where I want to pursue you to find out if this is a good thing between us or just a thaw after a long cold winter."

She chuckled thinking he was trying to see if there was

anything between them, and while part of her was curious and even wanted to seek him out, the other part was trying to run like hounds were chasing her.

She was tired of men pursuing her only to break her heart. Maybe for once she should be the one who left for a change. But did she want to risk that she would know when to leave before she became hurt?

"I'm an old maid."

"Honey, from my angle, you are not some old dried up maid. The frost hasn't even begun to shine on you. If anything, I'm the one who should be concerned. I'm chasing a woman fifteen years my junior."

She gazed at him, admiring the tilt of his chin, the way his dark eyes twinkled with a smile. Every time she looked at him, she felt her lips turn up in a grin. He made her laugh, he sparred with her, and she gave it right back to him. But a future? With Cal?

"You've finally gone riding with me. Was it that bad?"

She gazed out at the countryside, knowing she would never have gotten this scenery from the house. "No, Cal, the view is gorgeous, the ride fun and the company entertaining. It's one of the best outings I've had since I arrived."

He smiled. "I knew you'd like it if I could just convince you to get on a horse."

"It wasn't the horse that was holding me back; it was you. You're a temptation I don't need."

He stepped closer to her and for a moment she thought he was going to kiss her and she wasn't ready to experience his lips.

"Edwina, I haven't courted a woman since my wife. I don't even know how any longer," he admitted.

"And I don't want to be courted," she said. "That's why I've been resisting this attraction."

He reached out and caressed her cheek. "When Ida died, I sworn I'd spend the rest of my life alone."

"And I've been jilted three times. I don't want anything else to do with men."

"But there is something between us," Cal said.

"And we should ignore those feelings and walk away," Edwina said, wishing he would kiss her, leaning toward him.

"But we won't, will we," Cal said gazing down at her.

She chuckled instinctively knowing he was right. "Not on your life."

He grinned. "We better get back before we get into trouble."

"I think we already are," Edwina said and turned to walk back to her horse. "But I get the feeling, I think it's going to be a fun kind of trouble, until one of us gets hurt."

Cal helped her back onto her horse, the feel of his hands around her waist warm and tingly. Heat and desire flowed through her blood wanting more with Cal, needing him to touch her, but she refused. She broke it off because she feared if he kissed her, they wouldn't stop until they were both naked in the sunlight.

Cal led the way back to the ranch below and they were silent on the trip back. The horse ambled along, swaying her in the saddle almost rocking her into a peaceful lull. She'd known she would enjoy her ride with the handsome cowboy, but she hadn't expected to have thoughts of the two of them naked in bed, his lips moving over hers. She wanted more with Cal and that shocked her.

When they rode up into the yard, Cal came around and helped her off the horse, placing his hands on her waist. He set her on the ground in front of him and she didn't want him to release her, but he did.

"Would you do me the honor of letting me beat you at chess tonight."

Laughing, she couldn't help but admire the audacity of the

man. "Letting you beat me at chess? Never. I will meet you after dinner and show you no mercy as I annihilate you at chess, which by the way, I detest. It's just a strategy game."

She'd learned the man's game in boarding school. Women were instructed to let men win, as a stroke to their fragile egos. Edwina hated losing and refused to let her suitors have the upper hand.

Maybe that was her problem with men, she refused to give into to them and wanted a man to work for what he wanted. And none of her previous fiancés had needed her bad enough to fight for her hand. She glanced at Cal. Without a doubt, she knew this man would fight for what he wanted and protect it with his life.

For just a second, she wanted him to want her, but then she realized that was impossible.

"Other than checkers and poker, that's all the games I know." He winked at her. "I will meet you after dinner and show you who is champion chess player at the McIntire ranch."

"And if I win...I'll have to think up something for my reward."

He tipped his hat. "Tonight after dinner. You against me at chess."

"May the prettiest one win," Edwina said.

He laughed and started to walk away, he turned and grinned at her. "If I win, I expect a kiss."

"You're not going to win," she called, heat spreading through her like a wildfire. Why did she enjoy his company so much? And why could she hardly wait for tonight when she would win. But maybe she didn't want to win. Maybe she wanted him to kiss her.

❧

JESSE WORRIED when Pearl didn't come down to dinner. Edwina said she felt like she was coming down with a cold and after she'd fallen in the frigid waters of the river, he wouldn't be surprised.

While Edwina and Cal were playing chess and Grace was reading one of the books Pearl had given her, Jesse gave up resisting the urge to check on Pearl.

Picking up a bottle of sherry for her and for him a bottle of brandy, he hurried down the hill. The night was crisp and cool and the stars twinkled overhead like pin pricks in the sky. Moonlight guided him as he walked to the house where he'd been born and raised. The house had been plenty until he'd married Beth.

Walking up the steps, he knocked. Pearl opened the door, her hair loose, a shawl about her shoulders. She was beautiful and for a moment, he wanted to run his hands through her mahogany hair that curled down her back. Her nose was red and her eyes were watery.

"Edwina said you weren't feeling well. I was worried about you. Can I come in?"

She opened the entrance wider and he stepped through.

"Have a seat," she said, her voice deeper than normal. "I'm fine. Just a touch of a cold."

"I brought some sherry. I thought maybe it would help rid your system of the cold."

She shuddered. "I detest sherry. What else did you bring?"

"Brandy."

"That I would love to try."

He grinned. His first wife had loved sherry. But Pearl hated the stuff. That made him like her even more.

"You sit. I know where the glasses are."

Sinking down onto the couch, she pulled a blanket around her.

"When did you start feeling bad?" he asked walking into the kitchen. He noticed her makeshift mouse trap sitting in the corner, baited.

"Last night," she said. "After we returned from church."

Taking a tumble into a cold mountain stream was enough of a shock to her system it was a wonder she didn't have pneumonia. Though his back had been to the girls, he couldn't help but wonder if Grace had somehow helped her into the water.

He'd been shocked to see Grace's pet frogs being carried by Pearl. What had transpired between these girls and how had Pearl fallen in the river? Maybe he should ask her, but why hadn't she told him if his suspicions were true?

He walked into the living area, picked up the bottle of brandy and pulled out the cork. He splashed a healthy amount of the liquor into her glass and then into his. "Have you ever had brandy before?"

"No, do I need to worry? I just want something that will soothe the ache in my throat."

He handed her the glass. "Take a small sip at first and then another and soon you won't feel anything hurting your throat. Drink too much and everything will be numb."

She put her nose in the glass. "It smells delicious."

"I like it."

He raised his glass and clinked the side of hers. "To the suffragettes."

Putting the glass to his lips, he took a sip, letting the alcohol warm him from his throat to his stomach. He watched as she did the same, but she made a bitter face.

"That will take some getting used to, but I do enjoy the way it warms and soothes."

She laid her head back against the sofa and closed her eyes.

"So you're a suffragette. Since we're drinking alcohol, I guess you're not one of those teetotalers."

"That's the Women's Temperance Union. We split off from them years ago."

She was so beautiful sitting there with her head laid back against the sofa. He wanted to ask her questions, to learn from

83

her so he could understand what she was teaching his daughter. "So what is a suffragette? Explain to me why a woman who has everything would feel the need to join a movement where women are struggling to get more."

Smiling, she lifted her head from the back of the sofa. "First off, why do you think women have everything?"

"Because as men, we try to cater to you and make you happy," he said. He'd given his wife everything she wanted and it hadn't been enough.

"Then your wife would have been one of the lucky ones. But there are so many women who are abused by their husbands. They have no rights. The law doesn't care. Think about Grace. What would you do if you found out her husband was beating her? Could you just sit by and do nothing? Yet the law thinks he has that right because he's her husband."

Jesse would kill any man who harmed his daughter. Hell, he'd probably hurt them if they broke her heart, but to hit his little girl, he would not accept that. He knew men hurt women, but he'd never really considered it from the female's perspective. What choice did she have if the law did nothing?

"As a man, you have the freedom to come and go as you please. Women don't have that same privilege. Do you know what it's like for a single woman who tries to get a hotel room in a decent hotel, without a chaperone, is subject too?

"They investigate her to make certain she has a high standard of morality. Yet, if you were to bring in a paramour and rent a room, discretion would be applied and they would look the other way."

While he agreed that wasn't right and it was none of the hotel's business, he could also see that they wanted to make certain only moral women stayed in their place of business. But then again, if a man brought in a soiled dove, what was the difference?

"That's society. I agree it's not right, but there's not much you can do about the way society accepts women."

Shaking her head, she gazed at him, her brown eyes narrowing. "But it's wrong. Women should have the same rights as men. You have a child. What do you think would have happened if you'd deserted Beth, leaving her with Grace? The courts have the right to take away a woman's children. The father no, but the woman, they could take her babies."

He couldn't imagine anyone taking his child away. He'd even worried about Pearl somehow wanting to take Grace back to his wife's family. At eighteen, Grace could decide if she wanted to get to know her mother's family, but until then, no one was taking his daughter away. "That's barbaric. It's one of the reasons I love living in the west."

"Thank goodness many states are now listening and changing these laws. And then there is the vote. Why should we have to pay taxes, live within the elected laws when we don't have the right to cast a ballot and choose who we want to be in office. It's a pat on the head and the men will take care of it."

Picking up her glass, she took another sip. He smiled as he watched her. Talking about the women's movement had certainly inspired her as she sat up and suddenly seemed stronger.

"Don't women like men taking care of them? I thought that was what you wanted? Maybe that's why my first marriage was so troubled."

Beth hadn't wanted to make any decisions except where they would live. Even though when she met him, she'd oohed and ahhed over the fact she was dating a cowboy from Colorado. And he'd told her right up front he would never stay in Boston.

He'd been there on business and once that was completed, he was leaving with the intention of never returning. And then at a party the company he was working with invited him to attend, he met Beth and life had never been the same, for him or for her.

"Here's why I joined the women's movement." She leaned toward him. "My father was in charge of me, my trust fund, and made decisions about my life without even consulting me. Did you know back in the 1830s, a woman could not sign a will or manage her wealth."

Jesse couldn't imagine not being in command of his destiny. His father had let him decide what he wanted in his life and he'd had no doubt. The ranch.

"If I'd been born back then, my father would have had complete control. I would not have gone to college, but a husband-caretaker would have been found for me."

What would it be like to spend your life with someone you didn't love? He'd loved Beth, but known they weren't good for one another. Now her cousin was here sitting in the old homestead and he couldn't help but think while they were from the same family, she was different. A lot different from what he'd expected.

"My father is still trying to find me a husband, but I'm resisting. And while things have gotten better, there is still so much to be done to help women."

"So you're going to get your trust fund, set up a school to teach young women about suffragettes and never marry? What about children? Don't you want your own family?"

She picked up her glass and he poured more brandy in it. "Who is going to marry me and accept me as a partner, not a decoration who says yes to everything her husband tells her? I may be quiet, but when I speak, I want to be heard. You can tell me my opinion is not right, but you must hear me out and hopefully we'll make a decision together. How many men are willing to accept a wife who speaks her mind?"

She had a point. But most women wanted a family. Was Pearl so different that she didn't want or need babies?

"But what about children?"

Taking a sip of the brandy, she glanced down and then stared at him. "I want children. If I never marry, I will find orphans to educate and raise. I will have my own family with or without a husband."

Laughing, he laid his head back against the chair. "When I first saw you, I thought *oh she's not going to last*. But you know, Pearl, you're a hell of a lot stronger than you look."

"Thank you," she said. "What happened between you and Beth? I heard you two were happy. What went wrong?"

He snorted and held up his hand. "This is what happened. Coming back to Colorado, she hated living away from the big city. She missed the parties, being around people and her friends."

"But she never came home," Pearl said, gazing at him.

"No, she didn't," he said softly knowing there was so much her family didn't know. Things Pearl didn't understand, but he didn't want to talk about Beth. "How is my daughter doing?"

"She's a smart little girl. Sometimes I think she's too smart for her own good."

He sighed. "You'd tell me if she was causing trouble?"

The woman licked her lips. "She's a child. She's going to act out. If I can't handle her, I'll let you know. But I'm hoping to deal with it on my own, so she will begin to trust me."

So Grace was being difficult. "Don't wait too long to bring me in. I don't want you to leave because of my daughter."

She grinned at him. "So you no longer want to send me back?"

He avoided her question, not certain that he was ready to admit that his father had been right about his daughter. "Do you want to go back?"

"Not now," Pearl said. "I like it here. It's peaceful."

"I better go and let you rest," he said, rising from the chair.

"Oh, and by the way, how is the mouse situation. Is it getting better?"

"We're down to one a day. Hopefully soon, they'll be gone," she said, rising.

They were standing together, mere inches separated them and he could see the rise and falling of her chest as she stared at him. Warmth spread through him like the brandy they'd drunk, and his hands reached for her. He placed his hands on her cheeks and pulled her toward him. "I've wanted to do this since the day you got off the train."

His lips covered hers, so soft and firm, possessing her, branding her as her arms slid up around his neck and she settled between his legs. Kissing Pearl felt so right, he wanted to do more as hot, heavy hunger filled him.

He hadn't planned on kissing her and yet he didn't want to stop but knew this was suicide. His flesh was on fire for this woman and he knew this had to stop before it was too late. Slowly and reluctantly, he released his little suffragette. With his hands still on her cheeks, he knew he needed to step away and get back to the house, but he didn't want to go.

"I'm sick and you're kissing me."

"I had to," he whispered next to her ear.

She shook her head, her breathing labored. "We can't."

"Why not?" he asked, knowing he agreed but needing to hear her reasoning.

"You were married to Beth," she whispered. "You're still in love with her."

The urge to laugh was strong, but he resisted. He hated Beth for what she'd done to their family.

Stepping away, he glanced at her. "I stopped loving Beth before she left for New Orleans."

Pearl touched her lips with her fingertips and then gazed at him in surprise. "New Orleans?"

"My wife didn't like Colorado. She left me and Grace to go

to New Orleans," he said, picking up the bottles of alcohol. "Get some rest. I'll see you tomorrow."

⚜

EDWINA WALKED UP to the bigger house. Why she'd agreed to play chess with Cal she didn't know, especially since she detested the game. It was an irritating game of strategy. Maybe she could teach him Rummy or maybe they would just enjoy each other's company.

But why was she here? She'd given up on men after her latest disaster. Cal was a fun diversion. Someone to play with while she was at the ranch, but just as soon as she could, she was hopping on the next train to San Francisco. It was time to live her life the way she wanted, out of the control of her brother.

An owl hooted in the dark and she glanced around. She wasn't afraid, she was enjoying her stay on the ranch. It was quiet and peaceful, and Cal kept things interesting.

Walking up the steps, she noticed him standing there waiting on the porch for her.

"Nice night," he said.

"Yes, it is. Am I late?"

"No, I just wanted to make certain you made it safe and sound. Would hate for a coyote to think you'd make a tasty meal."

This morning on the ride, she'd wanted him to kiss her, but here he was baiting her trying to get a rise out of her, well two could play that game and she was an equal opponent.

"He'd find out real quick that I'm not as sweet and luscious as I look," she said, giving him a knowing glance.

"Are you trying to warn me? Because I don't scare easy."

After three fiancés and numerous dates, maybe he'd do well to be on guard. She obviously had trouble with men.

She shrugged. "You've been told."

89

"I'm a man. I'm not afraid of a little thing like you."

"Why are you pursuing me?" she asked, standing on the bottom step looking at him. His chest was broad and she had the most incredible urge to lay her head down and rest there. It seemed like it would be a safe place.

He smiled. "Because you tickle my fancy. You make me smile and you don't let me get away with anything. Now, get in here and let me beat you at chess."

"About that...I hate chess. What if we played a more challenging game of Rummy at a penny a point?"

He grinned. "I'll accept your challenge, but don't let my son know we're playing for money. He wouldn't be pleased if he knew we were gambling."

Part of her wondered how Jesse would feel about her playing with his father. After all, Cal had been widowed for several years, but still she wasn't much older than his son.

"I won't tell if you won't."

"He's gone down to check on Pearl. He was worried about her catching pneumonia after falling in the creek."

The man should be worried, his bratty daughter had pushed Pearl in. Edwina wanted Pearl to tell Jesse, but so far, she refused.

"Me too."

"Well, come on then, let me find the cards and we can get started before he gets back."

"What about Grace?"

"She's in her room playing with her doll. It's just you and me for a little while. It would be the perfect time for me to steal a kiss."

"And find yourself with a black eye," Edwina said, knowing she would love for him to kiss her, but she had to appear proper.

Why were these rules for women when right now she would like nothing better than to pull those full lips down to hers and kiss this man senseless. There was enough attraction flowing between the two of them.

But what if the kiss was disappointing? She'd been kissed by enough men to know that some kisses were tasty and delicious, and some were like warm mush.

Stepping up the stairs, she entered the house, and Florence, the housekeeper came around the corner. "Miss Grace is in bed."

"Thanks, Florence," Cal said.

"I'm leaving for the evening," she said, walking to the door.

"Goodnight," Edwina called and watched as the woman disappeared.

"Now we're alone," Cal growled, his voice deep and low, pulling her into his arms.

Her breath swooshed from her lungs as she felt her breasts crushed against his chest. Oh, why did this feel so good? Cal was a man—not the society weaklings she'd been pursuing. A man who would honor and protect her, and what was she thinking?

"I don't care if we play cards tonight. More than anything, I've been thinking about kissing that smart mouth of yours. You may give me a black eye, but it will be well worth the chance to taste those lips of yours."

Finally.

"Quit talking and get on with it," she whispered, her breath coming out in a rush.

Call her a loose woman, she didn't care, but she wanted him to kiss her. She wanted to feel his mouth moving over hers. She wanted to compare how she'd dreamed it would feel to reality. And then she was going to get on that train to San Francisco. This would be her new life. Men pursuing her, she'd let them kiss her and then she'd move on, never developing feelings for any of them.

His lips came crashing down on hers, his hand holding her face as his mouth claimed hers. She'd never had a man kiss her so aggressively. She'd expected just a simple peck on the lips like she'd received from all the other men she'd ever kissed.

But Cal's lips branded her as his own. A fire began low in her belly and she felt herself sagging against his muscled chest, her body willingly giving over to him.

Suddenly he released her. He leaned back and stared, his breathing heavy. "I think we better get to playing cards or we're going to be in trouble."

"You are trouble, Cal McIntire." Edwina pulled herself together, her breathing fast, her body moving slower like she was walking through molasses. As fast as she could get her dead limbs moving, she walked into the parlor, needing distance from this man who'd awakened her spinster body.

At thirty-five, she was a woman who'd never experienced a man. She wasn't some young innocent and she'd given love a chance, but never found the emotion. Maybe it was time to experience life in every sense and forget falling in love.

Cal laughed. "You're right, Edwina. I can be a fun kind of trouble or just plain trouble."

Sitting across from Cal, she studied the man. She wasn't expecting roses and rings and forever after, but maybe it was time to end her curiosity and learn what happened between a man and woman.

She might never have another chance to learn and this man was certainly one she would love to experience that which ladies did not discuss. Now how did she go about telling him she'd chosen him to be the one to claim her virginity and would he accept her proposition?

Thirty minutes later, after Edwina had soundly beat him at Rummy, taken a quarter from him. She stood. "I better go."

"Can I walk you back to the house?"

"You going to protect me from the coyotes?"

"I would fight them off bare handed to save you from their ferocious bite, only to claim you for myself."

The man knew how to make a woman feel special. None of those smooth faced banker boys had left her breathing hard just from their words. She smiled and reached up and caressed the side of his face. "You know, Cal. I'm not good marriage material."

He took her by the arm and led her from the house. "Why not?"

She needed him to see the reality of her life. The way no man wanted her and never would.

"I've been engaged three times."

Walking down the stairs, he looked at her and grinned in the moonlight. "Three times. What happened? Why didn't you marry them?"

She laughed. "The first one, Paul, was killed in a carriage accident. I caught James kissing another woman, and well, Brad was secretly married."

Cal threw back his head and laughed. "I don't know whether to be scared or honored that I'm now joining a long list of men who have fallen prey to your spell."

How could she make him understand she was tired of men who promised her the world and then gave her nothing. She was done with marriage and courtship.

"Well, none of them have, you know...." she said flustered.

Cal stopped walking and turned to her. "Yes, I know you're an innocent. But I'm a little past the virgin stage in life. And that concerns me."

Edwina stiffened. He didn't understand and how could she put this to him delicately like a lady should. "And who said I wanted to get married. I'm a little done with the fiancé, planning a wedding, and all the arrangements. I'm going to take what's out there. If I want to kiss a man, I will. If I don't, I won't. I'm going to live an independent life without a man."

They started walking again. Cal was quiet. When they reached her door, he lifted her hand to his lips. "I'm fifteen years your senior. I've had my children. You're still young. You haven't had yours."

Edwina laughed while inside her heart was breaking. He'd kissed her and decided there was nothing there and for the first time in her life, she had felt more passion than she knew how to handle. But she was tired of being hurt by men. Damn them all.

She reached up and touched his face. "You kiss like the devil and could probably charm a woman out of her clothes. But I'm leaving just as soon as I find out when the next train to San Francisco leaves. I'm done with men.

"So don't worry your handsome little head about me expecting marriage or an engagement or anything else. But I want to experience what happens between a man and a woman with someone I choose. I'm choosing you. Think about it."

With that, she walked up the steps of the house, opened the door and left him standing outside, his mouth hanging open. Maybe now he'd get the picture.

CHAPTER 10

*T*he next day when Jesse brought Grace to the house, Pearl met him at the door. "Good morning. Do you think it would be possible for us three girls to go into town this morning?"

Jesse gazed at the woman he'd kissed last night. He'd tried to tell himself he'd just overreacted and that it was an urge he'd acted upon, but her standing there looking fresh as the dew on a rosebud caused a little hitch in his breathing. The memory of kissing those full ripe lips slammed into him and he had the most incredible hunger to do it again, right there in front of his daughter.

He swallowed and tried to push his thoughts away. "I'd rather one of us went into town with you until I'm certain you don't get lost. I can't go today. I'll ask Pa if he has time. If he can't, then I could go with you in a couple of days."

The thought of traveling to Russell Gulch, just him and Pearl, had his blood flowing straight to his groin. But that would be difficult to do without his daughter.

"All right, I need to pick up a few things at the store and I know you're busy. I'd also like to spend some time shopping."

He laughed. "There's not much shopping to be done in Russell Gulch."

She shrugged. "I don't need a lot."

Beth had always said she just needed a few things. With a sigh, he looked at the woman who he'd almost gotten entangled with. This was a great reminder of why they could never be together. She was from the same family as his dead wife who had thought shopping was a new art form.

Once a week, she'd gone to town, running up his bill at the mercantile with all kinds of frills that hadn't made her happy. Pearl would never belong here. He would be wise to remember that soon she'd return to the big city and all the fancy living she was accustomed to, leaving him and Grace behind.

"Just take someone with you," he said, suddenly wanting to get to the herd. Pearl was like Beth and he'd do well to keep that in mind.

"We're going to town instead of studying?" Grace asked, gazing at him. "I'd rather go with you Pa."

Grace would be in danger and he couldn't watch her and get the work done he needed to do today. There was no way she could go with him.

"Not today, pumpkin, we're moving the cattle up to a higher pasture. I don't have time to watch you."

Grace frowned. "Pa, you know I could help you."

"Not today, Grace. Stay with Miss Weare, but promise me you'll be nice." His daughter sighed dramatically, her eyes turning dark with anger. "No acting up. Now promise me."

Grace wasn't dumb, and somehow he thought she was giving Pearl trouble, but he didn't have any real facts yet. Just a father's intuition.

"All right. I'll go, but tonight you'll play checkers with me?"

"Okay, tonight we'll play checkers and you can tell me about your trip into town," he said, knowing he'd be exhausted, but he wanted to reassure Grace that nothing had changed between them since Pearl had arrived.

"Thanks, Pa," she said.

"Enjoy your day, but be careful," Jesse said, wishing he was going with them, but knowing there was nothing he could do.

He didn't like the idea of the ladies going to town by themselves until he was certain Pearl could handle the wagon and knew her way back.

Hugging his daughter, he glanced up at Pearl and had the incredible urge to bring her in close for a hug as well but knew that was impossible. Sighing, he gazed at Pearl. He had to forget this infatuation for a woman who would hurt him just like Beth. They were alike, from the same family, and kissing her had been a terrible mistake.

"I'll ask my father to go with you and hitch up the wagon before I leave for the fields."

"I'd appreciate that," she said. "I'm sorry you can't go with us."

"Another day," he responded and turned and walked back to the house. He couldn't be around her. He had to distance himself or find her in his arms again. She was beautiful, she was smart. He liked Pearl, but she was also kin to his dead wife.

AFTER JESSE WALKED AWAY, Pearl took Grace by the hand. There were some things she needed to see about before they left for town.

"Come on, we'll meet Edwina at the wagon. Let's go to the house."

The little girl frowned. "Why?"

This wasn't going to be as easy as she'd hoped, but it had to be done if she wanted to keep Grace from being made fun of by the other kids.

Pearl smiled. "Show me your room. I want to make certain

you made your bed and see what books you have to read. We may need to pick up a new book."

Five minutes later, Grace was showing Pearl into her bedroom. "See, I told you I made my bed."

"You did and your room is nice and clean. Good job. Run downstairs and grab me a pencil and a piece of paper. I want to make a list of the books you have," Pearl said, thinking she just wanted five minutes alone to check out the little girl's armoire to see what dresses the child had in her closet.

"All right," Grace said, hurrying out the door and down the stairs.

It took less than a minute for Pearl to glance in and see two dresses that the girl had probably received before her mother passed away. There was no way the child could fit into the clothing. Quickly she glanced through the drawers and noticed no bloomers, no shifts, not even a nightgown.

When she heard Grace's footsteps on the stairs, she closed the doors and hurried over to the bookshelf where the child had her books, dolls, and several other toys.

"Here you go," Grace said, handing her a piece of paper.

"Thank you," Pearl said, quickly writing down the titles. "Have you read all these books?"

"No, ma'am," she said, glancing away. "They were my mother's. I really miss her."

Pearl stopped. It was the first time the girl had said anything about Beth. "I bet it's hard growing up without a mother in a house full of men."

The girl shrugged. The moment lost.

"Are you ready? We should be going if we're to get back before night fall," she told Pearl. Sometimes she felt like this child was older than she let on.

"Let's go," Pearl said. "You know, Grace, you should read one of those books. It might make you feel closer to your mother, knowing she read the same story."

"Maybe."

When they reached the front door, she saw Edwina and Cal standing in front of the wagon. Quickly, she turned Grace hoping she'd not seen the sight of the two of them, their arms wrapped around each other kissing in a way that looked sinful.

"Why don't you run to the kitchen to see if Florence has some cookies for us to eat on the way," she said, sending Grace away from the sight.

Stepping outside, she slammed the wooden door and the two of them jumped apart. "We're ready to go. Lots of things to take care of while we're in town."

She frowned at her aunt, who raised her brows, before letting Cal help her into the wagon. Why did she have the feeling this trip was going to be a trying experience in more ways than one.

❧

PEARL HAD Mr. McIntire drive her to the telegraph office where she went in and had a telegram sent to her trust manager. Not only had she sent a telegram to the lawyer in charge of her fund, but Edwina's as well.

It was time they took charge of their money and made their own decisions without the help of her father. On the way out the door, Cal shook hands with a tall man.

"Mr. Russell, good to see you. How's your wife, Helen?" Cal asked.

"She's doing very well. We're excited to be expecting our first child."

"Congratulations." Cal moved aside. "Let me introduce you to Miss Pearl Weare. She's here teaching our Grace. She was Beth's cousin. And this is Miss Edwina Weare, her aunt."

"Nice to meet you, ladies. Where are you headed next?"

99

"We're on our way to the mercantile to shop for books," Grace said.

"Great, you may run into Helen. She was going into the store this morning to do bookkeeping."

"I hope we meet her," Pearl said.

"Enjoy your trip into town, ladies. Cal," he said, tipping his hat.

The man walked down the street into the mine office, and they hurried to the wagon.

"Now you've both met the man who named the city Russell Gulch."

"He seems nice," Edwina said, sitting beside Cal on the wagon seat.

Cal clicked to the horses and they rambled down the road toward town. When they arrived, Pearl had Cal drop them off at the mercantile. "Mr. McIntire, why don't you meet us back here in two hours and then we'll grab a bite of lunch at the cafe before we head back."

"All righty," he said. "I'll give you girls time to get your shopping done."

After he'd helped the three from the wagon, he climbed back up and waved as he rode off.

Edwina put her hand on Pearl's arm. "I'm going to take a little walk around town. See what is here."

Pearl put her hand on Edwina's and squeezed it. "Okay, we'll meet you at the cafe."

"See you there," she said.

Standing in front of the door, Pearl took Grace by the hand. "Let's go inside and see what they have."

She'd been to Russell Gulch twice now, once coming through the small town and then again for church. But she had yet to go inside the mercantile and she could see from the outside it was nothing like the shops in Boston. But she would make do with what the small town had. Unlike many women, she didn't like spending a lot of time searching for that perfect dress. She liked pretty and functional, that was all she needed.

When they walked inside, it was clean and bright, and a woman approached them. "Welcome, I'm Helen Russell, how may I help you?"

The woman's face was thin, but she had the most beautiful pale blue eyes Pearl had ever seen on a woman and a smile that was warm and welcoming.

"I'm Pearl Weare, Grace's cousin. I'm here as her teacher for the next few months."

The woman was expecting a child and she seemed to radiate with happiness.

"You're married to Mr. Russell, the owner of the mine?" Pearl asked. "We just met him going to the mine office."

"Yes, Michael is my husband, and as you can see, we're expecting our first child."

"Congratulations," Pearl said.

"Nice to meet you. If you need any help, let me know."

"We're going to look around," Pearl said, pushing Grace in front of her.

"Where are the books?" Grace asked. "Miss Weare needs more books."

She really didn't. She'd brought almost a trunk full, but what she wanted to look at was the children's clothing, but first she had to ease into a discussion of clothing.

"The children's books are against the back wall," Helen said.

Grace tugged Pearl's hand pulling her to the wall. "These look pretty boring."

"I don't know. Have you read Tom Sawyer? It's the story of young boy living on the Mississippi river."

Grace's eyes widened. "Are there pirates?"

Pearl smiled. "No, but it's a fun book. He and his friend get lost in a cave." She picked up the book. "It's a little above your reading level, but I think it would be a great challenge for you."

"Have you read it?"

Pearl's weakness was books, and this was a good story she'd read over and over. And the author, Mr. Twain, had not failed to deliver a good adventure.

"Several times."

"What do you like about it?"

"I enjoyed Tom. He went from quite a rapscallion to a good young man."

The little girl picked up the book, turning the hardback over in her hands almost reverently.

"Do you want to read it?"

"Yes," she finally said.

"I'll buy it for you if you agree to a new dress and pantaloons."

Her eyes narrowed and she realized she'd been tricked.

Grace put the book back. "I don't want to read the book. I have dresses."

Pearl shrugged. "That's fine, but you've grown since those clothes were bought and they no longer fit you."

The child frowned and Pearl knew she'd tried them on. "I don't need a dress."

"You'd look like the other girls in church. You wouldn't stand out."

Grace rolled her eyes. "Those girls are milksops. I can ride a horse any way I want to. Pa said I don't have to wear dresses."

How could she help this child? She had to somehow make her fit in better with the other girls or they would ridicule her until her spirit was broken. She just couldn't watch them hurt Grace again.

Pearl put the book back. "He's right. But sometimes it feels good to fit in and not be made fun of. It's not nice, but those kids will continue to pick on you because they're afraid of you and jealous that you're not like them. I think you should wear your pants and ride your horse however you want when you're at the ranch, but when you go to church, wear a dress."

The child glanced at the book again. "There's a cave in this book?"

"Yes. It's one of my favorites."

Frowning, she stared at Pearl. "I don't have to wear a dress around the ranch? Just when I go to church?"

Pearl felt her heart skip a beat. The child was considering the dress. She knew she wanted to look like the other girls but was resisting because of her father.

"Yes," Pearl said, watching the child trying to decide.

"And you'll buy me the book?"

"Yes," Pearl promised. "And you get to pick out the dress."

The little girl wandered over to where there was a rack of dresses hanging. She looked at each and her eyes grew large as she held up a light blue dress that had piping along the bodice. The dress was pretty and Pearl knew she'd look adorable in the outfit.

"You want to try that one on?" Pearl asked, holding her breath.

"Yes," Grace said.

Pearl glanced up and saw Helen watching them with a smile on her face.

"Is there some place Grace can try this on?"

"Back here," Helen said, pointing to a room with a door. She opened the room and Grace glanced at the dress and then at Pearl.

"Try it on," Pearl encouraged.

The girl walked in and shut the door.

Pearl sighed with relief. The battle wasn't over, but the first skirmish had been won.

"Let me know if you need help," Pearl said through the door.

"Oh my God, I never thought I would see this day," Helen said with a laugh. "That child has resisted pretty clothes for as long as I've known her. I didn't know if it was because of her mother or her father."

Nodding, Pearl smiled. "I watched some kids pick on her at church and couldn't stand it. I don't think Jesse has bought her a single dress since her mother's passing."

"He hasn't here at this store."

The door opened and Grace walked out in the dress. She spun around. "It's really pretty."

Helen smiled. "You look adorable. There's a mirror here, if you'd like to see."

Walking to the mirror, Grace's eyes widened as she stared at herself. "I look so different."

Pearl hurried over and checked the fitting. The skirt went almost to the floor. "You're beautiful in pants or a dress. But now you look like all the other girls."

"Do you think Pa will like it?"

How did Pearl respond? She didn't know how Jesse would react to learning she'd taken his daughter into town to buy her new clothes. From what she gathered, he feared his daughter was going to become like his wife and so he encouraged her to look more like a boy.

The child was being raised by men who wanted to either forget or pretend that she was a little girl. And Grace was suffering because of their neglect. Because of her father's own fear of her being like her mother.

"I'm certain he will," she said, not wanting the girl to realize that her father liked her being dressed as a boy.

"Now, let's find you some pantaloons, a chemise, and what are you sleeping in?" Pearl asked, suddenly wondering if her father had purchased her any clothes.

The little girl shrugged. "One of Pa's old shirts."

"Would you like a nightgown?"

"Is it soft?"

"I'm sure we can find you one that's very soft."

Grace sighed. "Sometimes Pa's shirt is itchy."

"Well, let's look and see what they have. And how about boy's pants? Do you need more of those?"

She wanted to reassure the little girl and make her feel she wasn't trying to totally change her, but when she began to be comfortable in her new clothes, then maybe she could slowly ease her out of the boy's clothing.

The child shook her head. "No, I have lots of those."

For the next hour, they finished picking out new pantaloons, a frilly shirt that Grace insisted on wearing, a nightgown, chemise and finally, the book.

Pearl was uncertain how Jesse would react to his daughter's new found enthusiasm for shopping and little girl's clothes, but today she felt like the two of them had made progress.

CHAPTER 11

*E*dwina walked down the street of Russell Gulch looking around, biding her time for Pearl to convince Grace she needed a new dress. It was a pity her father and grandfather hadn't realized the child had no girl clothes, but then again, they were men raising a little girl.

At the mine office, she'd picked up a schedule for the train in Denver. But she wasn't quite ready to leave just yet. She was enjoying flirting with Cal and had yet to get enough of the big cowboy.

Yes, he was quite a bit older than her, but he was fun. And right now, she felt the need to enjoy life. She'd given up her dreams of a husband and family and was trying to adjust. When she arrived in San Francisco, she would seek out a different kind of life.

One where she lived a more bohemian style. Wine, men, friends, and whatever else she fancied at the moment. She'd given her brother's way of life a try and nothing had worked out.

When she left Russell Gulch, she'd begin on a new journey of fulfillment. Just as she passed the saloon, Cal stepped out, saying goodbye to a pretty woman.

"Good day, Becky Lee, thanks for everything." He reached up and pecked her on the cheek.

When he turned, he saw Edwina and his face turned red.

"Cal McIntire?" Edwina glanced between him and the woman. The lady gave her a coy look and then shut the door. She tried to hurry on past him, but he took her by the arm and placed her hand in the crook of his elbow.

"Edwina," he said calmly. "It's nothing."

"What's to explain? I just caught you coming out of a place of...of...wearing a smile."

Cal threw back his head laughing, which only infuriated Edwina more. She'd caught the man visiting a calico cat and he was laughing about it?

Well, she'd certainly misjudged his character and he was just like the other men who'd courted her. Who was she kidding? Cal didn't want to court her. He thought there was too many years between them. He'd said so last night, even after she'd all but promised him her virginity.

What had she been thinking? Cal had seemed like the perfect man to have a quick fling before she went off to her new lifestyle.

"We're friends, that's all," he said softly. "Nothing else."

"I offered you my innocence and...and you're..." She couldn't say the words.

He stopped and turned to her. "Listen to me. Becky Lee is a friend. I'm not the kind of man who would visit her and be with you. Maybe you've had that kind of man in your past, but I'm not that way. Especially if we're going to be together."

She stared up at him. "You're going to do it? You're going to end the waiting?"

An ache centered in her chest and she held her breath anticipating his response.

"I'm still thinking about it. But I got to thinking about what you said last night. Women are curious creatures and I never thought about what it would be like never to know."

She smiled at him and felt heat flood her body. While he was giving this a lot of consideration, she could tell he really wanted to be with her. And she wanted to experience a man. A real man.

The sight of Pearl and Grace leaving the mercantile, sent a shiver of fear through her.

"Cal, promise me that my niece will never know what happens between us. She would never understand, and she'd be quite angry with me."

"Promise me my son will never know. He'd be angry as well. He'd think I was being disrespectful."

They grinned at each other. "I do."

Grace started running toward them, her hands full of packages. "Grandpa."

"Hi, buttercup," he said. "What all do you have here?"

"Me and Miss Weare, we bought me a new dress and," she giggled, "some unmentionables. I'll show them to you when we get home."

Pearl walked up to the two of them, the fullness of her skirt, billowing around her.

Cal glanced at Pearl. "Did you ask my son if she could have a new dress?"

Buying Grace a dress was a subject she'd not discussed with the handsome man because he was afraid she would turn Grace into someone like his wife Beth. Funny thing was she hadn't even liked her cousin Beth all that much. The woman had been a pompous girl that snubbed her nose at Pearl and her beliefs of women suffragettes. She'd called Pearl foolish.

"No, Grace saw a dress she liked. Should I have asked him?"

"He's awful funny about Grace. Very protective of her."

"That's why he didn't notice the kids making fun of her at church."

᭡

JESSE WORRIED all day while he was out working the cattle with his men about the ladies and if they'd found their way into town. Even though his father had gone with them, he fretted about their safety. They were new to Colorado and not aware of the dangers in the area. And his daughter was with them.

When he came in that evening, he was bone tired from a day in the saddle and frankly he wanted nothing more than to grab a quick bath, some supper, and be off to bed.

But he'd promised his daughter they would play checkers and he wouldn't disappoint her. So after supper, they would have a quick couple of games and then he'd call it a night. Tomorrow he would be moving more cattle, but Grace would be learning from Miss Weare here on the ranch. He'd feel better knowing he could reach them quickly if needed.

He had to keep thinking of her as Miss Weare, Beth's cousin of that uppity Boston family that he never wanted any part of ever again. He may not be as wealthy, but he was no pauper by any means.

In fact, his spread was one of the most prosperous in the state. His father had started the ranch and now he was leaving the running of the McIntire land to Jesse while Cal considered running for state senator. He'd only mentioned it to Jesse, no one else. If Mick came home, he knew his father would run for office.

Seeing the wagon in the barn, Jesse felt relief. They were home. After he'd unsaddled is horse, he walked toward the house, ready to clean up and see his daughter. As he passed the homestead, he looked for Pearl but didn't see her. Maybe she'd be at the house as well and the thought warmed him. What would it be like to be greeted by a wife and child each night after a hard day?

Quickly he pushed the thought away. The auburn haired, brown-eyed vixen who suddenly filled his thoughts more than she should was too much like his wife. He had to remember she would never make him a good partner.

"Pa, Pa," he heard and looked up to see his daughter running toward him in a dress.

The sight of his beautiful daughter felt like the wind was knocked from his lungs as she ran to him. Her blond hair was long and flowing past her shoulders and the dress she had on made her look older, more mature. With a sudden glimpse into the future, he froze.

Rage burned inside him. She was seven, not eighteen.

"Pa," she twirled in front of him. "Look at my new dress. Pearl and I picked it out. What do you think?"

He wouldn't crush his little girl's soul, but he wanted to scream *take it off. You're much too young and it makes you look like your mother.* But he kept his silence, biting his tongue. Finally, he was able to control the anger pulsing inside him.

"I think it makes you look beautiful. But what was wrong with the pants you wear around the ranch?"

She kicked a rock with the toe of her boot. "Nothing. I like them, but I'm the only girl who wears pants to church."

"But you're the prettiest girl in pants," he said, trying to make his daughter feel like it was still all right for her to dress like a boy.

He knew the day would soon come for her to dress and act like a young woman, but he wasn't ready to experience his little girl growing up. And he didn't appreciate that either his father, who had been harping on getting Grace out of pants, or Pearl helped his daughter buy a new dress. She had dresses in the armoire she could wear to church.

"Oh, Pa, you're supposed to say that."

"I wouldn't lie to you. You're the prettiest girl there."

"But I'm the *only* girl in pants."

What could he say? She was right. He'd never thought it could do any harm, though his father had been telling him it was time for her to start acting like a young woman. She was getting too old to be traipsing about dressed like a little boy. Yet, keeping her in boy's clothing also kept her from growing up, and that's what he wanted the most.

"Who bought you the dress?" he asked, wanting to know who had intruded on his right to buy his daughter a dress when he was ready for her to start wearing them.

"I picked it out and Pearl helped me find the undergarments that I needed," she said quietly.

She helped his daughter buy pantaloons? What else had she bought his daughter? This was why he didn't want anyone from Beth's family near his Grace. Beth had run up a considerable bill at the mercantile and now it appeared Pearl had done the same. Once again, he realized that Pearl and Beth had a lot in common.

Another reason not to be with Pearl. He had to keep reminding himself she was like his wife.

"Do you like it?" he asked seeing her almost giddy.

She smiled at him the same way that Beth used to, and fear pounded through his veins.

"I love it. It's so pretty," she said, twirling around again.

"Then I'm glad you got it," he said, knowing it was a lie, determined that this was the last time that Pearl would turn his daughter into a girl, especially a girl like her mother.

"Are we playing checkers tonight?"

"After supper, but first where is Miss Weare? I need to speak with her."

There was a lot he needed to say to this woman.

"She's at the homestead."

"Thanks! Now you run up to the house and tell them I'll be

in just as soon as I finish talking to Miss Weare," he said, thinking this would be a short, conversation that might end with the woman packing her trunks and heading back .

THE TRIP into town had tired Pearl more than she expected. She wasn't quite over the cold she'd gotten when Grace had pushed her into the river. But today's excursion into town seemed to have brought them closer.

After her initial reservations, the child had seemed excited by the dress she'd found. And a few minutes ago, she'd watched Grace as she greeted her father in her new outfit.

From the window, she'd seen Jesse ride in, looking fine sitting that horse, his hat shading his face, his muscles rippling as the horse trotted into the barn. There was something about him that when she looked at him, she wanted to peel his shirt from his shoulders and explore the flesh hidden beneath his clothing.

She'd never thought about a man like this before and she was shocked at the scandalous thoughts where he was concerned. That kiss the other night had left her restless, unable to sleep, and Jesse never far from her thoughts.

A sudden pounding startled her, and she opened the door. Jesse strode in not waiting for her to invite him inside the house.

"Why in the hell did you buy my daughter a dress?"

Shocked, she stared at him. He was angry, furious, that she'd bought Grace a dress?

"If I wanted her to dress like a girl, I would have taken her to the mercantile myself and bought her clothes. I don't need you to be filling her head with all kinds of high society ideas of how a woman should dress and act. My daughter is not going to be influenced by your family and turn out like her mother, a rich society woman who didn't fit in here," he said.

He was right, Beth had been a snob from almost the moment she'd been born, but that was put there by her mother and father, not Pearl's part of the family, and she wasn't teaching Grace to be a snob.

She was trying to protect her. And it was ridiculous he would accuse her of teaching his daughter to be a rich society woman. No girl she ever educated would think that way.

"You're right. Beth was a snob. But I'm not teaching your daughter to be anyone but herself. But she's still a little girl and I felt sorry for her when I witnessed the children making fun of her at church for dressing like a boy," she said, standing her ground, wrapping her shawl around her shoulders.

He stopped and glanced at her. "What? What are you talking about? I never saw the children making fun of her."

"That's because you weren't paying attention. She was the object of their ridicule and she tried to hide her embarrassment. She didn't want you to know."

His body sagged and she could see the anger drain from him, but she wasn't through. Now she was furious. Several times, he'd made disparaging remarks about her family and Grace being a part of them, and she was tired of it.

Jesse ran a hand through his hair and licked his lips nervously. "Grace has dresses she could have worn."

Pearl had reached her limit. "Have you checked her dresses to make certain she can still wear them? When was the last time you bought your daughter pantaloons? A nightgown? Shoes?"

He frowned at Pearl. "She is not neglected if that's what you're getting at."

The man didn't even realize his daughter's clothes no longer fit. The only clothes that fit this child were the pants and shirt he'd bought her to look like a boy.

"She's outgrown everything. The only thing that fits her are the boy's pants and shirt and the boots she wears around the ranch. Nothing that was made for a little girl fits her any longer."

"That can't be right. We just bought her clothes..."

She watched as he realized how long ago those clothes were purchased for his daughter.

"I didn't mean not to buy her clothes. I just never think of needing that stuff since she wears boy's clothes all the time."

Jesse was in such a state of denial and doing harm to his child.

"She's growing up, but that doesn't mean she's going to become Beth," Pearl said, anger almost spewing from between her lips. Her fists clenching at the thought of how he wanted to suppress his only child.

"I know you didn't want me to come here and teach your daughter, but I'm not trying to take her away from you. If anything, I'm trying to help you make her into a young woman who makes decisions on her own, who has an education and won't let people take advantage of her."

Pearl took a deep breath and released it slowly, letting her anger drain from her.

"I don't want her to be like her mother. I want her to be Grace—no one else. She and I made a deal today. She's going to wear her dress to church, but the rest of the time she's to continue dressing like a boy until she decides to start wearing dresses. I'm hoping that now she'll be accepted by the other children."

Last night, they'd been kissing and today they were arguing. Maybe she should leave. After this argument, she doubted he would let her stay.

Jesse sighed, ran his hand through his hair and glanced at Pearl. "Boy, I didn't see that one coming. I didn't even notice the other children were not accepting her. I feel terrible she's been hurt because of me."

His forehead gathered together. "You're right. I fear she's going to become like her mother and I probably go too far the opposite direction trying to make her different."

Shocked, she realized he was admitting to fearing she'd become like his late wife.

"Just let her be Grace - not Beth or even yourself. She's never going to be the son you don't have. She's always going to be a girl and someday she's going to want to embrace her feminine side."

His eyes widened and he stared at her like he was truly seeing her for the first time. Shaking his head, he sighed and walked to within inches of her.

"The reason you're here is my father's attempt at making me realize Grace was growing up and not in a good way. I didn't want to have anything to do with the Weares after Beth." He took a step closer to her. He reached out and touched her cheek. "But you, you're different. I keep comparing you to Beth, and even today, I expected my bill at the mercantile to be run up when I saw Grace's dress."

"I paid for the dress. It's the least my father can do," she said.

"I'll pay you back."

"No, you're paying me a salary for a job I won't even be here that long for."

Lifting her chin, he gazed into her eyes. "I keep trying to remember that. But I can't help it. I want to kiss you. Even when I was angry earlier, I wanted to kiss you the moment I walked in that door. There are so many reasons why I shouldn't, but all I can think about is how I want to feel your lips against mine."

She licked her lips, his words causing her heart to pound in her chest, just as his mouth covered hers. How could she feel so angry at him one second, and the next, he was kissing her and she was loving the feel of his mouth consuming hers. Of the way his tongue slipped between her lips and caressed the inside of her mouth, pulling her body in close to his.

Her arms slipped around his neck and she pressed into him, enjoying the strength of his chest, his sinewy thighs and his belt against her stomach. She couldn't think of anything else, she couldn't imagine how being in his arms could be any better. All she could think about was the rush of heat surging inside her, filling her with a passion no kiss had ever incited before.

Never had she wanted a man to pick her up and carry her into the bedroom and for them both to shed their clothes. Never had she even considered that act with any other man. So what was it about Jesse that had her dreaming of the two of them naked in bed together?

She pushed her hand against his chest and broke the seal of their lips. "We can't. I'm leaving and you don't like my family."

He laughed. "You're right. But at this moment, none of that matters."

"What are we going to do?" she whispered, leaning her forehead against his chest, wanting to experience more in his arms, knowing that wouldn't be possible.

"We're going to enjoy our time together. Would you go riding with me tomorrow afternoon?" he asked.

Her heart skipped a beat. "I'd enjoy that very much, but what about Grace?"

"I'd like to spend some time with you," he said against her hair.

"I'll work with her in the morning, and then tomorrow afternoon, you can show me the ranch."

"I'd like that very much."

He walked out the door and she felt like her heart was going to pound out of her chest. Jesse McIntire was a man who made her think of home and heart and all the things she'd never desired before. But being with him would mean the end of her dream.

CHAPTER 12

$\mathcal{P}$earl could hardly wait for the morning to end. Going riding with Jesse, the two of them alone, was exciting and frightening at the same time. Exciting because she'd be spending more time with this big handsome cowboy and frightful because she'd be alone with this man who somehow awakened all her senses.

Today she and Grace were working on writing. The girl was having trouble stringing sentences together and they were composing a letter to help her learn how to write.

"Who would you like to write a letter to?" Pearl asked.

The little girl thought for a moment. "Grandmother Weare," she said.

"I think that's a wonderful idea. I know they would love to hear from you," Pearl said, knowing that Jesse would think she'd been the one to suggest it when his daughter was curious about her mother's family. "But why don't we start out with someone closer. What about your grandfather Cal?"

The girl giggled. Since the shopping trip, she'd been open and receptive to learning, and Pearl hoped they were now making progress, and this wasn't just a temporary lull before she returned to the imp who'd pushed her into the river.

"Grandpa's funny. I'll write him a letter," she said, picking up her pencil to begin to compose her sentences. Every little bit, Pearl would read it and then help her rearrange the words until they were finished.

"All right, read me the letter," Pearl said as she began to pick up the books and paper.

Dear Grandpa,

I am writing you my first letter because I love you. You taught me my letters and numbers and now Miss Weare is helping me learn more good stuff. Soon I will be as smart as you. But I will never be as old as you are. I miss Grandma but know she's in heaven with Mama. Love, your Granddaughter, Grace McIntire.

Pearl smiled. It was such a sweet letter, and she knew Grace was a loving child that could be stubborn to a fault, not unlike her father. At the thought of spending time with Jesse, a thrill spiraled down Pearl's spine as she dreamed of the coming afternoon.

"That was excellent. It's so good that I'm going to let you have the rest of the afternoon off. You may take your letter to your grandfather if you'd like," she said, picking up the books and putting them into her education trunk sitting in the corner. "How far have you gotten in Tom Sawyer?"

"I'm to the part where he talked the kids to paint the fence."

"This afternoon would be an excellent time to read. Then tomorrow you may read out loud to me."

She frowned. "What are you doing this afternoon?"

Pearl realized that Grace would be most upset if she found out that the two of them were going riding without her. "I have plans."

The child's brows drew together in a way that let Pearl know she was a terrible liar, even to a child. A knock sounded. She hurried over to answer the door, her full skirts swishing as she walked past the furniture. Opening the door, she caught her breath at the sight of Jesse standing there, a picnic basket in his hand, staring at her. "Are you ready?"

"Grace is still here," she said, trying to silently warn him with her eyes. One thing about Jesse McIntire, he was oblivious to how his daughter responded to the people around them. Pearl could see the storm brewing in the child's eyes, her father unaware.

"Where are you going?" Grace asked, her voice rising.

"I'm taking Pearl on a riding tour of the ranch and a picnic," he said.

Pearl could see the excitement building in the child and how her father had no clue saying no was going to upset her. And then Pearl would have to deal with the consequences tomorrow.

"I'll go saddle my horse," Grace said, heading for the door.

"Not this time," he said. "Pearl and I are going alone. We're going to spend the afternoon riding the ranch. I'll see you later this evening."

His daughter stopped and her big blue eyes widened as she crossed her arms over her chest. "I want to go."

She'd never witnessed Grace having a fit because she didn't get her way and suddenly she thought she would see how Jesse handled his daughter's tantrum.

"Grace, this is adult time. I'll be back later for supper and we'll spend the evening playing checkers."

"I don't want to play checkers. I want to go riding with you and Pearl."

Pearl was tempted to say let her go but thought differently when she watched as Jesse tensed at his daughter's reaction.

"Grandpa is waiting for you. I'll see you tonight," he said, his voice taking an authoritative tone.

Grace glanced at Pearl sending her a furious glare. There would be repercussions Pearl knew. The girl would not forget this betrayal anytime soon. Grace stomped from the house, slamming the screen door behind her as she went.

Jesse shook his head and turned his attention to Pearl. "Are you ready?"

"Just let me get my shawl," she said, picking it up on a hook near the door.

⁊⁊

CAL HAD NOT BEEN able to sleep all night long. Edwina's confession of being a virgin and wanting some lucky man to take her innocence had shocked him. In fact, he'd laid awake wondering why a woman would do such a thing and thinking about her reasoning.

She said she was never going to marry. She said she didn't expect marriage from Cal. But was that really true? How many decent women fornicated with someone and didn't expect anything in return?

But what about going through life and never experiencing that special bond between a man and woman. Their courtship, their marriage, their wedding night and eventually the family they'd create. She wanted to eliminate everything but the wedding night because she thought there was no hope for anything else. Could he give her what she wanted and walk away?

Oh, he was known as a flirt, but he'd loved his first wife and been lost since the day she died. Sure, he passed the time flirting with women and even occasionally visiting a saloon girl, but he'd never dreamed of helping a woman lose her virginity for all the wrong reasons.

Walking down the hill to the homestead he'd built for his first wife, he spotted Grace marching toward him, a frown on her face, her mouth pinched together like she'd eaten sour berries.

"Grandpa, you're watching me this afternoon. Pa and Miss Weare are going riding."

"And them leaving you here has put that terrible pinch in your mouth? You're ruining that pretty face of yours with that look," he said, knowing his granddaughter was upset.

She had never had to share his son before and Cal could see the sparks flying between Jesse and Pearl, and it appeared his son, for the first time since his wife left, was entertaining a woman. Just like he was on his way to entertain Miss Edwina without the accompaniment of his granddaughter.

"I wanted to go," she said with a pout.

"You know your papa never has time to himself or with a lady friend. Maybe you should be grateful he's getting time to do what he wants," he said, wishing his granddaughter had brothers and sisters. Hell, he'd wanted more children than his two sons.

"Humph," the child said.

"I'm on my way to visit with Miss Edwina. What are you going to do?"

"I'm going to go read," she said with a sudden twinkle that could only mean trouble shining from her eyes.

Somehow he got the feeling she was up to no good. He could see the mischievous wheels turning in her brain and that frightened him. "Now, Grace, I'm trusting you to behave yourself. Your father won't be gone long, and neither will I, but in the meantime, you're going to act like the young girl I know you're becoming."

"Sure, Grandpa," she said as she continued walking to the house, shaking her head. "I'll be glad when those two ladies are gone."

Cal knew he couldn't be gone long or there was no telling what kind of mischief she'd get into, but for now, he was visiting Edwina.

Hurriedly, he raced up the steps to the house he still loved.

The big house was Jesse's creation; this one he'd built. Knocking on the door, he heard her footsteps on the floor and then there she was. His heart leaped into his throat. She was as pretty as a picture hanging on a wall and she liked Cal enough to want him to introduce her to lovemaking.

His chest tightened.

"Cal, I didn't know you were coming over today," she said.

"Well, I came by this morning to ask you to go riding, but you weren't around." He cursed. "And by golly, Edwina, I laid awake all night long thinking about your proposition. My mind is just racing trying to decide if I should accept or say no."

She smiled. "I'm glad to hear you're considering it."

He pulled her into his arms. She fit right beneath his chin. She was such a small, petite woman and the men in Boston must've been crazy not chasing after her. If he were ten years younger, she wouldn't be able to run fast enough.

His lips covered hers and he loved the way she seemed to melt into him, her body soft and willing against his own. Her lips were like satin as he sought to let her know he wanted her so badly, he could barely wait. But they had to.

Releasing her lips, he stroked her face. "Do you know what you do to me? I'm not supposed to feel excitement like this for a much younger woman."

"I don't understand why you're concerned about our ages. Many women my age marry older men. And I'm not wanting to marry. I'm done with all that."

Or so she said. He'd yet to determine if that was real or just reckless bravado.

"Because..." he ran his hand through his hair, "you tie me up in knots, Edwina. I keep telling myself I'm a crazy old fool for even considering what you're asking. You're young, beautiful and I'm an old widower who never planned on marrying again."

He'd thought about it while he rumbled around in that big ole lonely bed of his. Something about taking her innocence and never marrying her bothered him. Edwina was not a loose woman. She deserved a man to marry her, just not him. He'd had his chance.

"We can't do this," she said, stepping out of his arms.

"Why not?"

"Because, I am not interested in marriage. I'm giving up on it and living my life the way I want. I don't expect anything from you."

Cal stepped away from Edwina and gazed about the house that was small. "How is it you want to live? That seems like such a questionable statement. It tells me nothing."

Really, he was trying to understand what she wanted. What did she expect out of life?

Edwina walked away and turned her back to him. "I've been searching for love and marriage for the last fifteen years, and frankly, I'm tired of the chase. My brother has introduced me to countless men who either never interested me or bored me with their pedigree. There's been continuous blind introductions of men he thought were eligible. I'm sick of this marriage merry-go-round. I'm going to San Francisco."

"What are you going to find in that wild, wicked city?"

"When I get there, I will find a small apartment and maybe even a job. There is nothing there I'm driven to do, just the chance to have peace. If I live a meagerly, I should have enough in my trust fund to let me live a normal, happy life. One without a husband and children, because obviously I'm not meant to have that dream."

This happy-go-lucky life sounded like one that would do nothing but get her into trouble. One where there would be no male around to protect her. But she wasn't his responsibility.

Cal shook his head. "You're not that old. You could still have a chance."

"No, I don't want another chance at any of it. I'm tired of being treated like a pawn in a chess match. My brother making moves that he thinks will increase the value of my portfolio, never considering the damage he's doing to my heart. If I go to San Francisco, he is on the other side of the continent. He can't get to me."

Now Cal understood she was doing this to get away from her brother. Constant introductions to new men must grow old for a woman. The disappointments must be heart breaking.

"Maybe you'll meet someone in San Francisco."

"No, I'm not going to get involved with society," she said, stepping closer to him. "It's okay if you don't want to do this. I just thought you were the right man since we seemed to be flirting outrageously with each other."

"I like to flirt, but I've been married. I loved my wife and I miss her," he admitted. "I still dream about her and when I wake up, I realize she's gone."

Edwina laid a hand on his arm. "I'm sorry. That must be hard."

"We're taking a huge risk here and I'm not so certain either one of us have thought this out."

His insides felt as if they were being ripped apart. How could a man turn down an opportunity to be with a woman like Edwina, but Cal wasn't a man who could just have sex and walk away. Even the soiled doves he'd remained friends with, just not lovers.

Edwina stepped to the window. "The only one really taking a risk is me. I could lose my reputation if anyone found out. No one thinks badly of a man, just a woman for not waiting for that magical day she's tied to a man forever. Like that will solve all her problems. So tell me, are you going to be the one who lets me experience lovemaking or do I keep looking?"

Shaking his head, he laughed. She was the one taking all the risks and he was such an old fool. He could talk about being with Edwina all day long, but he knew if she wanted him, he was not going to turn her down. And the thought of another man who might hurt her made him angry. "You'll look no further. I'm the only man who will help you. But after it's over we both walk away."

"Absolutely. When?"

"Just as soon as that son of mine and Pearl disappear for a few hours. We'd go to town, but the gossips would have no need for telegraph lines burning up with the news."

"We'll do this very soon."

PEARL SAT in the side saddle, riding alongside Jesse up into the foothills surrounding them. He'd shown her several of his pastures and now he was taking her to a higher elevation where the cows spent part of the summer.

"How big is your ranch?" she questioned, glancing at the man riding his horse next to hers. She loved hearing him talk about the land. She could see how he felt about the McIntire ranch and knew that Beth was a fool if she thought she could get him to leave this life behind.

"It's close to a thousand acres. My father was one of the original settlers out here and he's been adding to his holdings for many years."

"Do you like living here?"

"Oh yes. I tried several other areas and came back just as soon as I could."

He didn't say the words, but she knew he'd gone to Boston, but only stayed long enough to marry her cousin and then return with his wife at his side.

Her horse stumbled on a rock and she patted her on the neck. "Easy, girl."

Finally they reached a bluff that overlooked the valley below. "That's beautiful. I can see the house from here."

The big house sat at the end of the main road and then the

smaller cottage down around the side. It was a gorgeous ranch and she'd grown to love the whisper of the wind in the pines and the way the birds twittered outside her window each morning. She'd definitely miss this place when she left.

He smiled. "And this is where we're going to have lunch."

Swinging his leg over the horse, he slid to the ground and then came around to help her alight from the saddle. Placing his hands on her waist, he lifted her down. They stood there a moment, staring into each other's eyes. Her stomach rumbled.

"Sounds like I need to feed you."

"I'm a little hungry," she admitted, enjoying watching him tether the horses, his arms flexing as he tied them up.

"Good, Florence fixed us cold fried chicken with green beans from last year's garden. Along with her delicious sugar cookies," he said.

A cool breeze blew through the trees, sending a shiver through her. "Are you cold?" he asked.

"Not cold. Chilled. I'll grab my shawl."

"I brought a couple of blankets, so if you need one, let me know."

Jesse unhooked the basket from his saddle and then removed two blankets from his saddle bags. He took her hand and Pearl felt a rush of awareness spiral through her as he led her to the edge of the bluff and spread the blanket. She knelt and unloaded the basket.

"Have you ever brought anyone up here to have a picnic?" she asked, regretting the words even as they left her mouth. It wasn't that she was jealous, just making conversation and that's what her mind came up with.

"No, you're the first," he said. "Beth and I met in Boston and married there."

"Yes, I remember you eloped and then her parents threw you a party," she said. "I thought maybe you might have brought her up here after you were married."

Pearl didn't want him to realize that the reason she hadn't attended their wedding reception was because she didn't care for Beth. So she'd been busy that afternoon. Now it seemed like a petty thing to have done, but at the time, she was tired of Beth making fun of her beliefs.

"Oh no, Beth was pregnant by the time we arrived from Boston. She hated being with child, her body changing and growing. Then after Grace was born, she did better. She loved the baby and took good care of her until she was almost three. Suddenly, she was bored. By this time, I'd built the house and I thought we were happy. But she needed to be around people, the city."

If Beth's parents knew that she'd left her husband, they never said a word. None of the family had known she'd gone to New Orleans.

Pearl took out the metal plates and handed one to Jesse. She unwrapped the food and put some on his plate. "How long had she been in New Orleans when she died?"

He sighed and stared into Pearl's eyes. "Two years. There were grand parties and she was tired of living on a ranch in the frozen north."

"That must have hurt that she would leave you and Grace."

"I loved Beth. I tried to make her happy, but nothing I did satisfied her. She needed the type of life I wanted nothing to do with. I don't like big cities, parties, and social functions. I've attended several and frankly, I don't find them enjoyable."

He looked out over the land. "This I love and if I had it my way, this is how I would take my last breath. Sitting up here on the bluff, looking down at the land I worked all my life."

A breeze ruffled her hair and she watched as a hawk rode the wind, searching for his next meal. Nothing could be more wonderful than this moment with this man in such a beautiful setting.

"It's gorgeous here."

He hung his head. "Pearl, I really like you. But you come from the same family as Beth. I'm not willing to take a chance on another woman living here and being miserable. So whatever is happening between us, you have to know I will never marry."

She realized there was no hope of anything happening between them. Their dreams didn't seem to mesh. She wanted to build a school and he would never leave Colorado.

"Understood. And you, Jesse, have to understand, I have plans. I'm waiting to hear back from the trust manager about my trust fund. Once I have that money, you'll need to find another teacher for Grace. I'm going to make a difference in how the next generation of women are educated."

He laughed and picked up her hand. Setting his plate down, he pulled her close, needing to feel her body next to his in the only way they could ever experience. "We both want the same things in different ways and yet I can't get you out of my system. You're always on my mind. When I see you, I want to kiss you and when you're not around I dream of kissing you."

"So kiss me and know that soon I'll be gone," she said softly.

He lowered his mouth over hers, dragging her onto his lap, his lips ravishing her. She moaned deep in her throat and the sound made blood rush straight to his groin.

Why with Pearl did he want to forget all his promises, his vows of abstinence and make love to her? Why with Pearl did he forget the bad times with Beth and long to make Pearl his own? And yet they both said this was just a summer romance and once Pearl could, she would be gone. And Jesse would return to his life that he loved, lonelier than ever.

PEARL TRIED all morning to teach a sullen Grace who wore anger like muddy cowboy boots, noisy, pointy, and leaving tracks everywhere she went. She'd been disagreeable, disruptive, and almost belligerent.

Even when Pearl had tried to talk to her about her anger, she'd put her fingers in her ears and refused to listen. Finally, Pearl told her one more outburst and she'd not only make her do extra work, but she'd also discuss her behavior with her father by marching her home.

After that, the child seemed to settle down and they'd finished the day on a bright note when Grace had read the next chapter of Tom Sawyer aloud and had done excellent. Her reading had improved so much over the last few weeks that Pearl knew she'd soon be reading adult books.

"I'll see you tomorrow, Grace," Pearl said, as she walked her to the door. "You did very well today."

"Thanks," she said and walked out the door. She skipped around the corner of the house and disappeared.

Letting out a sigh, Pearl hurried out the back of the house to the outhouse. Cringing, she went inside the outdoor bathroom. Sitting there, she suddenly felt the building rock. "Hello?"

Silence.

Finishing, she pulled her skirts down and reached for the knob. It wouldn't budge. The door was jammed. She pounded on the wood frame. "Hello? Is anyone out there?"

Silence. Then she heard a giggle and knew. Grace had locked her in the outhouse. "Grace McIntire, let me out right this minute."

No response.

"Edwina," she screamed. "Jesse?"

Nothing. Heat begin to build in the small building, and she shuddered. She hated using an outhouse and missed the inside plumbing of the homes in Boston. At least there, someone would have heard her. A fly buzzed her face and she batted it away.

She'd done everything she could to make Grace like her, but

she was done. This time she was going to have it out with that child and she would be punished.

Pearl was done being nice. She didn't care if Jesse got mad, fired her, or sent her back to Boston. Pearl had had enough of one small little girl.

A rat ran across the floor and Pearl felt her heart leap into her throat. She screamed and pounded on the door. Mice she could handle, but this was a rat and he was looking at her like he was hungry.

"Let me out of here," she screamed and pounded harder.

"Pearl, hang on," Jesse called. She could hear him running. "Where are you."

"The outhouse. Hurry, there's a rat."

She heard him removing whatever was blocking the door and then he was pulling her out of the building, into his arms. "Who put the board against the door?"

"Grace," Pearl said, hanging onto Jesse, loving the way his chest felt against hers. "I'm sorry, Jesse, but I'm not putting up with her anymore."

She released her arms from around his neck. "Where is she."

"I'm right here," she said softly.

They both turned and stared at the girl. She'd seen them— Pearl hanging all over her father. She knew they were...whatever they were doing. It wasn't courting, even Pearl didn't know how to describe what was going on between her and Jesse except that she liked the way he made her feel. And she liked Jesse for the man he was.

She walked over to the little girl. "Grace, did you lock me in the outhouse?"

The girl glanced at her father and then back at Pearl. "What if I did?"

The child was almost daring her to say anything, like she knew her father would defend her. Not when he learned every-thing she'd done.

"You've been upset all day that I went riding with your father without you but locking me in the outhouse is not nice. You've put frogs in my bed, switched the sugar and the salt, pushed me into the creek and now this.

"Tomorrow morning, when you come into the schoolroom, you will bring me a piece of paper that says, 'I will respect others, including Miss Weare.' I want that sentence written three hundred times."

The girl's eyes widened. "Three hundred times. That's a lot of paper."

"That's a lot of time as well," Pearl said. "I suggest you get started."

Jesse stepped up to his daughter. "You will clean the horse stalls for the next week. I suspected you were causing trouble but had no idea how much. Now march on up to the house and we are going to have a little talk. I'll meet you there."

He'd guessed all along, but hadn't said anything to her? That was disappointing, but then she remembered he had asked her, and she'd wanted to handle Grace all on her own. It was just as much, if not more, her fault.

"What are you going to do, kiss her?" Grace asked.

Pearl watched as Jesse's face turned a brilliant shade of red. Oh, that poor child may be cleaning horse stalls until she was twenty-one if she wasn't careful.

"Get to the house, Grace," Jesse demanded in a voice that Pearl had never heard from him.

After his daughter walked away, her shoulders dejected, he touched Pearl on the elbow. "Why didn't you tell me? Why didn't you let me know she was misbehaving?"

He did care. And she should have included him in her decisions, but she wanted to appear like a strong teacher in control.

Pearl sighed. "Because I wanted to handle it my way first without going to you. I was hoping she would accept me, and we'd be just fine. And now that she knows we have feelings for one another, she's going to feel even more threatened. You've been the mainstay in her life for so long."

"I know. But her behavior is unacceptable," he said, running his hand through his hair. "This is when I wish there was someone to help me be a better parent. To show me where I'm failing and strengthen me," Jesse said, gazing at Pearl.

For a moment, she wanted to be that help mate. "But you're afraid that woman wouldn't like living out here in this beautiful area. Of being isolated from people."

"Because Beth was that way."

"Not every woman you meet is going to be like my cousin Beth," she said, thinking of how much she had enjoyed living on the ranch. "Do you think I'm like her?"

He stared at her for a moment. "I did when you first arrived. But you're different. I just fear that you too would get tired of living without the society that Boston has."

She laughed. "Usually, I'm the gossip of society functions. I avoid society as much as possible. They're a very boring crowd and I prefer the company of Twain and Shakespeare and Alcott."

"Who are they?"

"Authors I love to read."

"Oh," he said.

"You should try one sometime. Even your daughter is reading Twain."

He sighed and glanced toward the house. "I better go deal out some fatherly punishment." He reached out and touched Pearl on the cheek. "Wish me luck."

She smiled. "Good luck."

He walked toward the house and she knew that tomorrow Grace would be a better student, because the girl didn't like disappointing her pa.

PEARL

JESSE KNOCKED on the door of Grace's bedroom.

"Come in," she said softly.

He walked in glancing around the room his wife had created for his daughter. Beth had been an excellent homemaker sending off for decorations, buying when they went into Denver and decorating the house with next to nothing. She'd had a knack for making a house into a home, except for the relationships with the people who shared that home.

"Pa, I'm sorry. I just got so mad that you went riding with her and not me," Grace said, trying to defend herself. "I wanted to go with you, not her."

His daughter had never had to share him with another woman. He'd always been there for her and maybe he'd spoiled her just a little. No, not maybe, he *had* spoiled her.

He'd felt guilty and thought it was his fault she'd lost her mother. But looking back, he realized Beth had made that choice, not him. She'd gone off and left their daughter here with him and he'd been doing the best he could. But he wanted to do better. And he had to start right now.

He sat on the edge of the bed. "You know, Grace, since before your mother died, I've been the one to raise you. To tell you when you mess up and point you in the right direction.

"Your grandfather was the one who tried to make me realize you needed a woman around. Someone to show you how to be a little girl and I didn't believe him. I thought things were going just fine. But since Pearl has been here, you've shown me he was right."

"No, Pa, no. I'll be good."

"It's not a matter of being good, Grace. It's more you need a woman to show you how to wear dresses when we go to church. You need a woman to help with your hair. You need a woman to be around and teach you how to behave. And I need someone to help me be a better father, because obviously I've failed with you. I thought you knew how better to treat people

133

with respect. My daughter has done hurtful things to a woman who is trying to educate her. Make you smarter than all the other kids in town."

Grace hung her head. "I only wanted to learn from Grandpa and you."

Shaking his head, Jesse felt like he was to blame for part of this. He was certain Grace probably overheard him and his father talking about how he didn't want a woman coming to teach Grace and his father insisting the child needed someone to educate her not only in reading and writing and math, but things a girl needs to know. Things that he and his father were unable to teach.

"And for a while, I thought that was best. But I don't believe that anymore. I didn't realize how much you've grown. How you're changing from a little girl into a girl on her way to being a young woman. And while I hate that my little girl is growing up, I also want her to be an educated woman who can take care of herself. I can teach you some things, but Pearl--Miss Weare, she can guide you in ways I don't know."

"But you know everything, Pa."

The girl knew just how to get to him. She'd already learned flattery and no one had taught her that feminine device.

He laughed. "Honey, I wish I did, but I don't." He picked up her hand. "Now, I want you to promise you will be respectful to Miss Weare while she's here. That you're going to learn from her and stop these mean, hurtful acts."

His daughter sighed. "All right, I will." Her brows drew together and he could almost see her mind churning with questions. "Are you going to marry her, Pa?"

The words all but slapped him in the face. Was this the reason she was acting out? Obviously, she'd seen the two of them together.

"No, I'm not."

"Then why were you hugging her?"

"There was a field rat in the outhouse that frightened her. She was scared and I was comforting her."

His daughter's eyes slanted, and he could tell she didn't know whether or not to believe him. "Are you going to kiss her?"

Grace was suspicious and he wasn't really ready to answer her questions. How could he say anything when he wasn't certain of what he was doing with Pearl? They were attracted, but he didn't trust her to be happy here in Colorado and she had a school to build.

"That, young lady, is a question you don't have the right to ask your father. Someday you'll understand."

She stared at him expectantly. Good grief, he had to get out of here or learn how to answer her way too observant questions better.

"You have a paper due to Miss Weare in the morning, so I suggest you get busy writing it. And the horse stalls need cleaned out. Any other disrespectful acts toward Miss Weare will result in you getting a spanking. And you haven't had a spanking in years. Are we clear?"

"Yes, sir."

"Good, then get busy. And, Grace, I love you. I probably don't tell you often enough, but I'll always love you and want the best for you." He hugged his daughter to his chest, knowing her sweet child's body was changing and this was the first of many trials for him as a father.

"Love you too, Pa."

&

TWO WEEKS LATER, Pearl sat beside Grace as she read from Tom Sawyer to her. In the last few weeks, the child's attitude had completely changed and her learning was surpassing everything Pearl could show her.

In math, they were up to division with her having conquered multiplication tables and even some fractions. In history, they were reading about the effect of slave trade and its part in the Civil War. And every day, they read a few more pages of Tom Sawyer.

Even Jesse was reading the book and talking to his daughter about the adventures of Tom and Huck. There had been no more incidents since the outhouse, and even the mice population seemed to have disappeared. Summer was at its height and fall was not far on the horizon.

With each day, Pearl seemed to settle into a nicer routine. The only person who seemed anxious was Edwina. There was something going on between her and Cal and Pearl didn't know what exactly.

They sparred like two kids and yet they flirted with one another, and several times, Edwina had returned to the house with her lips swollen. Yet, she refused to talk about her romance. She'd grown very secretive about Cal.

"That was the best you've ever read. Tomorrow we're going to start a new book. One I think you're ready for."

Grace hopped up and smiled at Pearl. "I know at first I didn't like this, but you're teaching things that Grandpa never could."

But Pearl felt like Grace was teaching her as well. She'd planned on running the school she meant to build, but never actually teaching. Now she couldn't imagine not being a teacher. And her father had sent her here in punishment, but she felt like she'd found her purpose in life.

Pearl smiled. "Go spend the rest of the day doing your chores and playing outside."

"See you later," Grace said, running out the door.

Pearl sat and rested for a bit. The girl was precocious and she was becoming quite fond of her. She hoped that Grace would grow into a woman who had control of her future, her destiny, unlike so many of her sisters before her.

With a sigh, Pearl stood and picked up the books, papers, and everything she'd used teaching. She was going to take a walk and then maybe write a letter or two.

A knock had her hurrying toward the front. She opened it hoping to see Jesse, but instead Ernie Smith stood there. "You had a telegram in town, ma'am. I thought it was important, so I delivered it to you."

"Thank you," she said. "I know we're a ways out of town. Let me pay you for your trouble."

"Thank you, ma'am," he said, waiting at the door while Pearl went to her reticule. Quickly she dug out some coins and handed them to him. "Again, thank you so much."

"Do you want me to wait while you write a reply?"

Still not used to being unable to walk down the street to the post office or the telegraph office, she nodded. "Just a moment."

She ripped open the envelope and read the words, her eyes widening with the knowledge. Anger shot through every pore and she wanted to scream in frustration, but instead she took a deep breath and went in search of a piece of paper and a pencil. Quickly, she scribbled the note to the lawyer.

She handed him the paper and smiled. "Again, thank you so much for bringing me the news. My response is in the envelope."

"Thank you, ma'am."

After the man left, she sank into the nearest chair. She felt so foolish for taking her father's word. He was more dastardly than she had given him credit. Her trust fund had been hers since she turned eighteen. He'd told her twenty-one. She could have already opened her boarding school if not for him. Now she had no reason to stay in Russell Gulch. Now she was free to go.

Why didn't that news make her feel more joyous? More excited? Because she'd begun to like the life she was creating here. She enjoyed Grace and Jesse. And now she would be leaving them on the next train to Boston.

CHAPTER 13

Jesse watched Ernie Smith ride away and knew that Pearl or Edwina had received some kind of message. He wanted to run over and ask, but knew it was none of his business. Pearl had to live her life and he had to live his, even though he wished there was some way they could work this out. But how?

She didn't want to give up her boarding school and he didn't want to give up his life here on the ranch, and well, he knew he'd never be happy living in a big city surrounded by people. Especially, her family. Beth's parents had approved of their marriage only because they wanted to settle their wayward daughter.

Later that evening, he walked over to visit with Pearl, unable to contain his curiosity, hoping she would confide in him, anxious to see her. Knocking on the small frame house his father had built, he wished he could go back in time and that he'd met Pearl first, not Beth. When she answered the door, she smiled at him and stepped out on the porch.

"I was hoping you'd come by tonight."

"Want to take a walk down by the creek? It's not completely

dark and the moon is shining brightly," he asked, knowing he really wanted to get away from the curious gaze of his daughter and kiss Pearl.

"Let me grab my shawl," she said, walking back inside.

Soon she came out and he helped her wrap the thin covering around her shoulders. He picked up her hand and tucked it into his arm, bringing her in close.

She smelled of lavender and roses and all he could think about was kissing her full lips until she was moaning in his arms. But that would have to wait. He didn't need Grace to see them kissing.

"How are you?" he asked, liking the way her eyes twinkled in the moonlight as she gazed at him. "Has Grace been doing okay?"

"Grace has been a star pupil these last few weeks. The girl is going to know everything I brought to teach her in record time."

He smiled. That's what he wanted to hear. How his daughter was doing wonderful and spending her time learning, not creating problems. Yet, in many ways, she was just like her father. He'd given his mother problems when she'd educated him to the best of her ability. "That's wonderful, Pearl. It's because she has such a great teacher."

Why did he feel like the message she received held news that wouldn't be good for him, but for her? He wasn't ready for Pearl to leave. Yet, he'd been the one to encourage her to contact the lawyer directly.

"Thank you, Jesse. It's funny, but I hadn't planned on becoming a full-time teacher and now I'm actually enjoying teaching Grace. You know I didn't want to come here. My father forced me because I was arrested for marching in a suffragette parade."

Shock gripped his chest, his mouth dropped open as he stared at this beautiful, innocent woman and laughed. "You were in jail?"

He couldn't imagine someone arresting this woman and putting her behind bars.

"Oh yes. They arrested over five hundred of us that day and I was included. My father was appalled and furious when he had to bail me out and pay the fine." She shook her head, laughing. "That's when he said, 'you're getting out of Boston for a while and I know just the place to send you.' And here I am."

One thing about Pearl, he could always depend on the strength of her convictions. She'd said she wanted to change the world and help women. Being arrested certainly was doing everything in your power to bring light to her cause. But he hoped he never had to bail his daughter out of jail.

He pulled her in tightly. "And then when you arrived, I didn't want you here. I didn't think you'd stay."

"No, you didn't."

"But I'm glad you stayed. These last two months have been good for Grace and for me," he said softly.

An owl hooted in the night and the water babbled over the rocks, a soothing sound.

She gazed around in the darkness and sighed. "I don't know why, there is something about this land that seems to soothe me and make me feel at peace with myself. Like there's nothing here I can't tackle."

The land did the same for him. It strengthened and gave him purpose and made him feel at peace.

"Even a grizzly bear?"

She laughed. "No, not a bear, but I find the solitude relaxing."

He shook his head. "In winter, being snowed in for days even gets to me. I think you, Miss Lawbreaking Suffragette, would be bored in no time."

"We get snowed in for days in Boston. And those are the days I enjoy the most." She shrugged. "As for being in jail, it's a creepy feeling. One that I don't want to experience again, even for the suffragettes. There are other ways to bring about change."

They continued walking, not saying anything. The silence between them felt strained for some reason and he didn't understand why. Before, they'd always been at ease with one another. Finally they reached a bench he'd built near the river where he liked to sit and think. Sinking down onto the bench, he pulled her in close to keep her warm.

"I received a telegram from the lawyer today."

His blood froze and he held his breath. Why did he have the feeling she was leaving?

"I could have received my trust fund on my eighteenth birthday. My father kept the information from me so I wouldn't have control of the money. I'm free to do with it as I please."

He knew that's what she wanted. He knew it was the best thing for her, but it wasn't good for him, nor for Grace.

"Congratulations," he said, wondering why he'd ever given her that piece of advice, but knowing it was for the best. He needed to get over her and she needed to follow her dreams. "So when are you leaving?"

She sighed and ducked her head. "I'll be leaving next week if you have time to take me to Denver. Don't say anything to Grace. I thought I would take her riding and tell her while we're out. I wanted her to hear it from me, so that I could tell her what a great pupil she's been and how she should continue her studies."

Not only was he losing a great woman, but his daughter would be losing her teacher. And while he hadn't wanted Pearl here at first, now he couldn't imagine life without her by his side.

In their short time together, she'd come to mean a lot to him.

"I guess I'll have to find someone else to teach her," he said. "But no one will do as good a job as you have. And no one will make me wish things were different and that we could be together. But you have a school to build and I have the ranch."

He lifted his hand and brushed a piece of hair away from her face. She gazed at him. "Do you still think I'm like Beth?"

For a moment, he simply looked at Pearl. "You're different but you come from the same family who is used to the highest quality, society parties, and not living isolated on a ranch."

"You're right. I'm from the same family, the same upbringing. Beth was the one who enjoyed attending parties and social functions. I was the more scholarly, the serious, girl in the family. My father complained you could always find me behind a book. And it was true. I wanted to learn what the world was about. And I never got along with Beth."

He shook his head and laughed. "All this time, I've compared you to a woman you dislike."

"Yes," she said softly.

He'd been so stupid. "I'm sorry, Pearl. You are nothing like Beth."

"Yes," she said, standing. "I think I should get back."

He wasn't ready to take her back. He wanted to kiss her, to hold her close, but already he could sense her withdrawing from him and that hurt. They still had a few days, why couldn't she let things remain the same until she left? But he knew it was best if they no longer kissed. It would only make it that much harder when she rode away.

PEARL FOLLOWED Grace as they rode from the house. She'd told her that since she'd been doing so well, she thought today they should take a break and go riding. Let Grace show her part of the ranch.

Grace had told her they would go pick huckleberries. Wanting to give her a reward for working so hard, Pearl had agreed, though in the back of her mind she recalled that Grace also told her the bears liked those berries and she wanted nothing to do with the large furry beasts. They could have all the fruit they wanted.

Riding alongside one another, Pearl stared out at the pastureland below them where the cows grazed. She could barely see Jesse's corn crop that he'd been working so diligently on this summer and any day they would be eating fresh corn. But Pearl knew she wouldn't be here to taste the succulent vegetable. She'd be on her way back to Boston and Edwina would be headed to San Francisco.

Part of her didn't want to go. Even if she never built her school, she knew it would be for the best to leave Jesse and Grace behind before her heart became even more entangled with the two.

Last night, she'd wanted to kiss Jesse so badly, but she also realized his kisses could be almost drugging, they were so good, and she feared being tempted to do something rash as to kiss him until they were both naked in the moonlight.

Yes, she was torn about leaving Jesse. Part of her said continue with her dreams and the other part felt like she'd come home. Like this was where she was meant to be, but Jesse hadn't proposed and she doubted he would.

Beth left him because of her dislike for living in Colorado and he feared Pearl doing the same. And if he believed she would leave the man she married, then he didn't deserve to be her husband.

The word *husband* radiated through her, warming her and filling her with a sense of peace and joy, and oh my God, had she fallen in love with Jesse? Could that be why so many feelings of uncertainty and despair were filling her? But what could she do?

The man would never ask her to marry him. He would never give her a chance, but always compare her to Beth. And she and her cousin were as different as a rose and a cactus. Both had thorns, but one you could live on and the other was just a bloom that would soon fade.

Sure she had feelings for the rancher, but had he captured her heart? No other man she had ever met made her feel special. Treated her with respect and listened to her like she had a great mind.

No man had ever raised feelings within her to the point she craved his touch, the sound of his voice, and his handsome smile.

Yes, she had fallen in love with the big man and would hate leaving him behind, but she couldn't stay knowing he would never return those feelings.

Sighing, she glanced around at the country and knew she could never return to Colorado because it would always remind her of Jesse. And he and the state would always own a piece of her heart. A tear rolled down her cheek and she quickly swiped it away.

"Are we almost there?" she asked Grace.

The girl turned around, her eyes all excited. "See those bushes coming out of the side of that mountain? That's where we're going."

"Good, I was starting to fear we were lost," Pearl said, trying to close her mind to thoughts of Jesse and love and enjoy this last afternoon with this beautiful little girl. Her heart sagged with the knowledge of what she had to tell her.

Ten minutes later, they arrived. Pearl jumped off her horse and pulled out the sack lunch Florence had prepared and a blanket to sit on. "What do you want to do first? Berry picking or eating?"

"Oh no, if we pick the berries we will need to be on our way as soon as possible. So let's eat our lunch and then we'll pick berries and go."

Pearl glanced around uneasily at the area. "You're sure we're safe here?"

She didn't want to end her time in Colorado with a run-in with the bears.

The little girl shrugged. "Usually Pa is with me. We just need to be extra cautious and make lots of noise if we see a bear."

Spreading the blanket on the ground, Pearl sat and Grace joined her. She passed the homemade sandwiches out. Pearl didn't know how to prepare the conversation she needed to have with Grace, but she wanted the girl to understand her leaving had nothing to do with her.

"Are you and Pa sweet on each other?" Grace asked, shocking Pearl.

What could she say? She didn't want to lie to the girl, but was it her place to say anything to the child?

"I like your pa. I think he's a great man."

"Are you going to marry him?"

They'd been so careful. Had the girl seen them kissing or how did she know they had feelings for one another. "No. He hasn't asked me to marry him."

"Do you love him?"

Pearl didn't know how to respond. She'd just realized she loved Jesse and she wasn't ready to tell anyone. Not even Edwina and most definitely not Grace. She glanced down at her hands and decided the best thing was to avoid the question. "There's something I need to tell you. But first, let's talk about your schoolwork."

The child frowned. "Am I in trouble?"

"No. In the last two weeks you've done exceptionally well. So good, that's the reason we're taking the day off from your studies. You've done well with everything I've shown you and soon you're going to be past the books I brought with me. Congratulations and thank you for working so hard."

"Yay," Grace said, clearly not understanding.

Now that she'd made the girl feel good, she had to rip her world apart and that made her sad. She'd loved this time with

Grace, even the part where she'd found frogs in her bed. She'd never forget her time here with her and Jesse.

"Since I'm out of books to teach you from and the fact you're doing so well, I'm leaving."

"Nooo," the child wailed, her eyes widening.

Pearl licked her lips and stared as tears welled up in Grace's eyes. What a difference from several weeks ago.

"I'm going to Boston to open up a boarding school for young girls. I'll be teaching them the same things I've taught you," she said, seeing the despair on the girl's face.

"I don't want you to leave. I started liking you and now you're going to leave me." The girl jumped up. "That's not fair," she sobbed.

Stomping over to her horse, she grabbed the reins.

"Grace, what are you doing?" Pearl asked, fear surging through her. Grace was acting irrationally.

"I'm walking out on you first. I don't want to pick berries with you if you're going to leave me. First my mother left, and now you're abandoning me. I was hoping you would be my mother."

She jumped up on her horse and Pearl suddenly realized she was going to be alone. She ran after the child, screaming, "Grace, stop."

Tears streamed down the child's face as she turned her back, kicking the sides of her horse, galloping away. The sudden motion of Grace's horse, spooked Pearl's animal and before Pearl could stop her, the mare took off racing away after Grace.

Pearl stood, the blanket on the ground beside her with the leftover lunch and nothing else. No water...nothing. She glanced at the sky refusing to let panic overwhelm her. She had about five hours of daylight left. Enough time for Jesse to find her if he realized she was missing. The wind whistled in her ears, reminding her she was alone. Totally alone. Except for the wildlife.

EDWINA NERVOUSLY STRAIGHTENED the small house. Not that there was much to tidy, but it kept her hands moving while she waited on Cal to arrive. Pearl and Grace were out of the house, Jesse had gone to the cornfield with the ranch hands and Florence was busy in the big house.

They were going to spend a few hours together, and by later this afternoon, she would have more than a working knowledge of what happened between a man and a woman. When she left for San Francisco, she could put all of this behind her and begin a new life without the constrictions of polite society.

A knock sounded and she hurried over to the door, her full skirts swishing. There stood the big handsome cowboy, grinning.

"Get in here," she said pulling him in. If her brother ever found out about this, he would make her and Cal's lives miserable.

"Well, hello to you, too, darling," he said in that deep drawl that rippled down her spine. This man was more irritating than a gnat in church and yet she enjoyed sparing with him, being around him, and knew that part of her could hardly wait for today.

"Are you certain, you still want to do this?" he asked, pulling her into his arms.

"Are you having second thoughts?" she responded.

"And thirds and fourths and fifths all with the thought that I hope she doesn't back out now," he said.

She smiled. "I'm not backing out. I feared you were."

"No," he said, his lips covering hers. With his mouth moving over her lips, her heart began to race and fear about what she was doing pumped through her veins. Why, when she kissed this man, did she feel this rush of warmth that went from her head and centered between her legs?

She'd never experienced such heat and desire before and it frightened and thrilled her at the same time. Did all women's bodies surge with wanting when a man kissed them? She never had before.

Placing her hand on his chest, she pulled back. "Should we talk about this some more? I mean--"

His lips covered hers again as he brought his hands up to her cheeks and held her mouth in place as he ravished her lips, claiming her, possessing her and she welcomed his lead. She had no idea what happened next, but whatever it was, she wanted him to continue.

He released her mouth and pulled her toward the bedroom. "No more talking, Edwina. I've been anticipating this day. It's time to make you mine."

Heat flooded through her and she willingly followed him, frightened, but certain of what she was doing. This was why she'd chosen Cal. She knew with certainty he would take care of her, protect her, and help her understand what happened between a man and a woman.

"Cal, you know I won't stop talking," she teased him as she hurried into the bedroom.

He walked in behind her and closed the door. "Oh, yes, you will. I know how to keep you quiet."

"Show me, Cal," she said softly.

AN HOUR LATER, Edwina lay in Cal's arms, her naked chest pulled tightly against his own, his muscled arm wrapped around her solidly as if he would never let her go.

She felt numb from the sensations she'd experienced in the last hour. As she lay next to Cal, she realized the reason she'd never done this with anyone else.

She'd never had emotions toward other men she'd dated.

She'd never gazed into their eyes as they made her cry out in passion and felt like she was connected to them both physically and emotionally.

Yet, Cal had said there would be no declarations of love and marriage. He'd made sure she understood he never intended to marry again. And she'd made him realize she planned to leave soon and she'd be traveling on to begin a new adventure in her life.

"Well, darling, what did you think," he asked. "You're awfully quiet."

"That's because I'm worn out, Cal McIntire. If you remember, you had me going," she said softly against his chest. She didn't want to lie to him, she couldn't, but she hadn't expected to feel so many feelings toward Cal.

She had foolishly thought she could do this and then walk away. And she would, but it would be the most difficult thing she'd ever done. She'd never intended to fall in love with Cal, but she had, and she knew he didn't feel the same.

"Are you okay? I'm kind of worried about you."

"I'm fine. I'd like nothing better than to fall asleep with my head on your chest."

He didn't respond and then his voice was gruff sounding, almost choked up. "It's a nice feeling. But I fear we're going to get caught if we don't get moving."

As if on cue, they heard shouting in the front of the big house.

"Sounds like trouble," he said, sitting up on the side of the bed, reaching for his pants on the floor.

She wanted to pull him back to her, to keep him in bed, knowing this would never happen again. This was the only time she would ever experience Cal's arms.

Tears burned her throat, her chest tightening with a painful sensation and she felt like a volcano about to spew as she almost choked on the bitterness of it ending.

The risk she'd taken was beginning to arise and yet she knew her heart was too involved and she had to somehow keep him from seeing how she was feeling.

She needed him to leave as soon as possible. She needed to be alone and let the tears building inside her release.

Quickly, he dressed and then he turned back to her as she lay in bed. "Edwina, I feel honored that you chose me. And I have to tell you I loved every minute of being with you."

Unable to respond without choking on a sob, she stared at him as he leaned down and kissed her on the mouth.

"We'll talk later," he said, and slipped out of the room. She heard the back door open and close and knew he was gone.

The tears she'd been holding back flooded her throat and she lay and sobbed.

Somehow, even though she'd promised herself it wouldn't happen, she'd done the worst thing possible and fallen in love with Cal McIntire. She had to leave as soon as possible. She had to pack and get away, because if she stayed, he'd see the emotion she was fighting. He'd know she'd fallen in love and that would never do.

CHAPTER 14

orking in the barn, hanging up and reorganizing the bits and saddles, Jesse couldn't help but think about Pearl leaving. He didn't want her to go. The woman was always on his mind, but since last night, she'd been his main focus.

His heart was aching with the knowledge she would no longer be here on the ranch and he knew that Grace would be upset when she learned of Pearl's departure.

But the woman had dreams and he wasn't going to be the one who kept her from obtaining what she wanted in life. In some ways, he still felt that by marrying Beth he'd ended her dreams of being a society hostess.

It was time to let Beth go. She'd been dead for over two years. She'd been gone from his life for five. For too many years, her memory had swayed his decisions regarding his daughter and even his decisions. He'd never considered remarrying and he'd always wanted his daughter to be the opposite of her mother.

And while he still hoped she would be different, he could never change her from being a girl. He needed to guide Grace but let her become her own woman. And to stop comparing her to Beth. After all, his daughter was part of him as well.

Hanging up the last of the bits, he watched Grace as she galloped into the yard of the barn. She'd been crying. Hadn't she and Pearl gone riding together? Running out of the barn, he hurried over to his daughter sliding off her horse.

"She's leaving," Grace cried her boots hitting the ground. "Did you know Pearl was leaving?"

"She told me last night," he said softly. "Where is she?"

"I got so mad, I rode off. I left her like she's abandoning me," Grace said.

Anger rose in Jesse unlike anything he'd felt since his wife had left. "How do you know she can find her way back? She doesn't know this area."

"All she had to do was follow me. Her horse knows the way home."

Pearl was alone in country she was unfamiliar with, trying to find her way back to the ranch. If he'd had the time, he would have spanked his daughter right then, but he had to get to Pearl before she became so disoriented, she was even harder to find.

And he didn't even want to consider the dangers she was in. He could only pray that God would keep her safe until he reached her side.

The horse that Pearl had been riding trotted into the yard.

Jesse cursed and his daughter's eyes grew wide.

"Where is she? She was supposed to ride home on her mare," the child said her voice trembling.

"Grace, you never go off and leave your riding partner. Now Pearl is out there with no ride home and only a few hours of daylight left. Get to the house and when I get back, you will be punished."

Jesse had no time to waste. Pearl was out there without a horse, miles from the ranch.

"I'm sorry, Pa. I thought her horse would bring her home. I never thought..."

"You didn't think is right. I'm going after her," he said, running into the barn. Quickly, he grabbed supplies, a blanket, a bedroll and a first aid kit. Throwing the saddle on the back of his horse, he quickly tightened the cinch. When he found her, they could both ride his horse. And he would find Pearl and bring her home.

His daughter was standing in the barnyard, tears streaming down her face. As much as it broke his heart, he wasn't going to comfort her, she needed to learn a lesson. She needed to think before she reacted to her anger.

His father came from around the back of the homestead and he stared at him. What was he doing behind the old homestead? Why wasn't he up at the house?

"Tell Grandpa what's happened. If I don't come back before dark, send someone looking for us in the morning."

"Let me go with you, Pa. I'll help you find her."

"No, you'll slow me down. Where were you?"

He wasn't about to take Grace with him. She needed to experience the waiting and worrying about someone's safety.

She hung her head dejectedly. "I took her up to where the huckleberry bushes are. We were going to pick berries."

For the second time that day, Jesse cursed. "Grace Diane, you know how dangerous that area is with the bears. You left her defenseless up there with the ripe berries."

"I didn't think about it, Pa. I just got so mad that she was leaving that I rode off."

She was a child, but still what she'd done was wrong and she needed to learn there were consequences. Now he only hoped there were no long-term ramifications that she'd never forget.

"When I return you will get a spanking for being so disrespectful and you will be cleaning horse stalls in the barn for another two weeks. Now tell your Grandpa where I'm going."

Pearl was in an area were wild animal food was plentiful, and with evening only two hours away, the bears would be coming to feed. He had to get there before she was in even more danger.

&

CAL WATCHED as his son rode off.

When he reached Grace, she was crying.

"What's wrong?" he asked, knowing something bad had happened.

"I left Pearl at the huckleberry bushes with her horse, but the horse just returned without her," Grace said, sobbing.

"Oh, Grace honey, do you hate the woman so much you wanted to kill her?" he asked.

"No, Grandpa. I want her to stay. I don't want her to leave," she said, turning her wet face up to him. "I never thought about her horse running off without her."

She sniffed and Cal felt his chest ache in sympathy for his granddaughter. She was a kid. And kids sometimes did stupid things. Even adults did stupid things.

Was letting Edwina get away a shortsighted mistake on his part? He'd just spent the most enjoyable afternoon he could remember with a woman who had sweetly given herself to him and he was going to let her go?

The thought of her leaving with Pearl next week had his old ticker aching like when his wife passed away.

Taking a deep breath, he tried to focus on his granddaughter. "I suggest when your pa brings her back, you meet her in the yard and apologize to Miss Pearl."

"Pa said I was going to get a spanking."

He sighed. He hated it when his son punished his grand-daughter, but he couldn't disagree with his decision. "You put

Miss Pearl in danger. She could be lost. She could get injured. Let's just pray your pa finds her before anything bad happens.

"I'm sorry, Grace, but you need to stop and think before you react. Now get up to the house and wait with Florence. I'm going to go tell Miss Edwina her niece is missing."

The little girl started crying again, but obediently walked toward the big house, her head lowered, her shoulders hunched together. God, he wished he could spare her the pain of making bad decisions, but it was just part of life. No one escaped a bad decision or two. Was his decision never to marry again a bad one?

He looked toward the house where he'd just spent the most pleasant hours he'd had in a long, long time. After Ida died, he didn't think anyone could take her place.

He never intended to become involved with another woman, but then Edwina had come into his life tempting and teasing. She was fun, so different from Ida, and yet she'd claimed his heart.

He'd been mistaken when he thought he could show her what went on between a man and woman and not have any feelings. He didn't like to admit his shortcomings, but Edwina had been so trusting, so giving, and today he'd shared not only his body, but his heart once again.

He didn't want her to leave. The only thing he wanted was to carry her into Denver and marry her. He knew she'd given up on getting married, but maybe she just hadn't found the right man and he wanted to be that man. He wanted to marry her, and he was going to ask her just as soon as Pearl was found.

With a determined stride, he strode to the homestead. Knocking on the door, he stood on the porch and waited. She didn't come to the door. He waited and still no response. Finally, he pushed open the door and walked in. "Edwina."

No answer.

He pushed open the bedroom door and there she was

dressed, packing her trunk. She'd been crying. "I didn't answer because I didn't want to speak to you or anyone else."

"You're packing."

"Yes, I'm leaving." He watched as her chin trembled as she tried to hold back the sobs.

Taking her in his arms, she resisted at first, and then she melted against him. "What did I do wrong? I've hurt you and I never intended to make you cry."

She sobbed against his shirt.

"Damn it, Edwina, those few hours in your arms have given me new life blood. I feel like I'm twenty, not fifty, and frankly, I love how you challenge me, laugh at me and make me feel good. It's like that missing part of me has been found and I don't want you to leave. My heart is yours for the taking."

He pushed her back, holding onto her shoulders as he stared into her lovely eyes, giving her his heart.

"I love you, Edwina. I know you've given up on men and marriage, but maybe you just hadn't found the right one. I know we made no promises to each other, but I can't do it. I know there are some years between us, but I don't care. Would you please marry me, Edwina?"

The next thirty seconds lasted a lifetime as his heart pounded inside his chest like a hammer banging an anvil. Did she love him, like he loved her?

She smiled. "That's why I was crying. I thought I could just have sex with you and then go on, but during all that sparing, I fell in love with you and today when we were together, I realized I loved you and I had to get away before you realized I cared."

She bit her lip and then sighed. "I remembered what you'd said about never marrying again and I knew I couldn't stay here without you realizing how much I loved you. Yes, you're older than me, Cal, but you're the only man who's made me feel strong and happy and so very cared for. Yes, I want to be your wife."

Cal slanted his mouth over hers and kissed her, his mind screaming at him he had to tell her about Pearl while his body just wanted to focus on what they'd shared.

He released her lips, kissing her softly again. "We'll go to Denver just as soon as things settle down and get married."

Now the part that he didn't want to tell her. He prayed that this day would not be ruined with a deadly accident. He was depending on the good Lord to make it so.

She gave him a funny look. "Things settle down. What's going on?"

He took her by the hand and led her into the parlor. He sat her on the couch. "It's Pearl, honey. Jesse's gone searching for her."

"What?" Edwina said.

Cal told her what he knew and he watched the anger come over her. "Now, honey, Jesse has already told Grace she's going to be punished for being disrespectful. But right now, he's out searching for her and he knows exactly where she is. My son cares more than he's letting on, he'll find her and bring her home."

He was praying his son would find Pearl. He'd seen the looks those two had been giving each other and he just prayed she was okay.

"Oh, Cal, that girl deserves some happiness. And Grace..."

"She's a child, honey. Kids do stupid things because they don't know the value of life. She's learning a hard lesson. She's up at the house crying because her pa was all over her about leaving Pearl."

"That's what all the screaming was about. I was so busy packing, I ignored the sound coming from the barnyard."

He hugged her to him. "Nothing bad is going to happen

today. I just know it's a great day because you agreed to marry me."

He hoped and prayed he was right because he didn't want the day he asked Edwina to spend the rest of her life with him to be marred by Pearl's disappearance.

She reached up and trailed her hand down his cheek. "I love you, Cal McIntire."

&

JESSE RODE the poor mare hard. He knew exactly where Grace had left Pearl and while part of him hoped she was waiting there for him to arrive, the other part feared she'd left the area to try to walk home.

Not knowing the direction, it would be so easy to become lost. Yet he also worried that with the berries bursting, she would be in danger of the black bears and even the grizzlies. He had to reach her.

His heart swelled in his chest at the thought of something bad happening to her. He didn't know if he could live with the idea of her being injured or killed.

Pearl was a unique woman. She was independent and wanted to teach young girls to be strong and self-determining. She was the type of woman he wanted his daughter to become. And he didn't want her to leave.

He understood why Grace had acted out, he wanted to lock Pearl up and keep her on the ranch, but that would not let her be the woman she was. That would not let her achieve her dream of opening a boarding school.

The mare stumbled and he slowed the pace. He didn't need for them both to be afoot. But there was something about the word *school* that nagged him.

Russell Gulch wasn't very big, filled with miners. A few had families, but it was growing. Michael Russell's wife, Helen was expecting their first child. One of the young boys who worked the mine had come to visit Pearl several times to borrow a book.

Any children born here would eventually need schooling and while Mr. Russell had yet to hire a teacher, what if Pearl built her boarding school right here in Colorado?

It would take some years to build up the clientele, but she could teach children the importance of learning and being independent, and he could teach girls the value of knowing how to shoot and ride and anything else they would need to be a partner in marriage.

Excited at the idea, he realized it would be a way to keep Pearl here and also help her achieve her dream. And he would promise her she would always be his partner, his helpmate and the love of his life. It was a chance they both could get what they wanted and still be together.

But did she love him? She kissed him like she cared, but did she love him enough to stay when the wind whipped through the trees, moaning under the onslaught of snow. When the cold seemed to seep into every crack and crevice in the big house and you awoke to a layer of ice on the water to wash your face each morning. Could she love him enough to stay even when snowed inside for days at a time?

His chest ached as he realized that since the day she'd arrived at the homestead, there had been that strong defiance that drew him to her. She had arrived determined to teach Grace and not only had she taught Grace, she'd schooled him in how he needed to put the past behind him and move on.

And then she'd shown him what a strong, independent woman she was and he'd been enamored almost from the first day, though he'd fought that attraction at every step, determined to never marry another woman.

And if Pearl would have him, he'd be the lucky one. Now he just had to find her before nightfall and the temperatures dropped too much. Before the bears came to scavenge for food. And then they would talk.

Ten minutes later, he heard shouting and rode in that direction, his heart pounding fiercely in his chest. Kicking the mare, he knew he was close to where Grace had left Pearl.

"Go away," Pearl screamed. "Get out of here."

Climbing the last bit of the hill, his eyes widened as a momma bear and her two cubs were not far from where Pearl had started a small fire. Brandishing a flaming log, she was shouting at the bears as he rode into view.

Jerking his pistol from his holster, he fired his Colt away from the bears, hoping the noise would be enough to frighten them away. The boom of his gun had Pearl glancing back, her eyes wide with fright. The momma bear took one look at him, roared, then she ambled off with her cubs following her. With bears fiercely protective of their young, he shivered as he thought of what could have happened if he'd arrived five minutes later.

Swinging his leg over the saddle, he jumped to the ground.

Pearl came running and flew into his arms. "I knew you would come."

Grasping her to his chest, thankfulness flooded him. She'd believed in him and knew he would come after her.

"Oh, God, Pearl, I've been so worried. I was so afraid. I'm so, so sorry and Grace will be disciplined."

She laid her head on his shoulder and shook in his arms. "I don't think she thought about my horse following hers back to the house. Yes, she meant to leave me out here, but not stranded the way she did."

She was defending his daughter and that made him love Pearl even more.

He squeezed her against his chest and kissed the nape of her neck. "Doesn't matter. She should never have ridden off and left you alone."

Jesse felt so grateful Pearl was safe; she was here.

"I never doubted you wouldn't come after me. I almost started walking, but I feared I'd get lost. So I decided to wait right where she left me."

"How did you build a fire?"

She smiled. "A college course I took taught us how to build a campfire without a flint. But I must say, it was extremely difficult." She held up her hands to show him the blisters and splinters where she had rubbed them raw generating the heat necessary to start a blaze.

"I hoped you'd be here before it became dark, but I didn't want to wait until then to try to start a fire. Plus, I hoped that maybe you'd see the smoke. And I thought it might ward off the bears."

He laughed, reached up and placed his hands around her face. He gave her a sweet kiss. A rustle in the huckleberry bushes drew his attention. "Come on, let's get out of here before that mama bear decides to come back."

Stepping away from her, he kicked her small fire out and then stomped the embers. It hadn't been much of a fire, but still it had been enough to help protect Pearl and at night it would have helped him find her.

He lifted her into the saddle, her dress bunching up in the back, hiking up and showing off her trim ankles and calves. If it wasn't late, he'd like to explore that further, but he had to get her back.

Once she was settled, he climbed on the horse behind her.

"Can the horse handle both of us?"

"We'll go slow and stop often to give her a rest."

Pearl turned and glanced behind her. "Someday I'd like to come back here when I can enjoy this spot."

"It's a promise," he said close to her ear, breathing in the scent of this woman he'd almost lost today. He didn't want to live without her. He didn't want her to go, but she had dreams.

As they plodded along, she leaned back against him, filling his soul with a warmth he couldn't remember ever experiencing. She was safe, and somehow he had to convince her to stay. He wanted her in his life.

"You know, Pearl, I think all of us have changed since you and Edwina arrived. My father is whistling again, and he hadn't done that since before mother passed away. Grace, oh my goodness, what can I say but that I've seen the rebellious side of my daughter, but I've also seen her taking a step toward becoming a young woman and while I wish she would stay my little girl, I'm so proud of who she is becoming. I know today was not a good example, but don't give up on Grace. She's back at the house worried sick about you, regretting her actions."

Pearl smiled up at him. "What about you?"

He laughed. She'd had a huge effect on him, and even today, he realized that he'd let his hurt and anger cloud his decisions for way too long.

"When you arrived, I didn't want you here. I wanted you on the next train back to Boston. And then you showed me how my daughter needed your help. How you weren't like your cousin. How I needed to get over Beth, and well, I'm no longer the same man. I think I'm a better person because of you."

It felt so good to admit to her that he'd been wrong and she'd helped him see a better future. A future he wanted with her by his side.

She reached up and caressed the side of his face. "Jesse."

They were at the bluff where they'd had a picnic. The sky was ablaze of orange backlit by blue. He stopped the horse and helped Pearl alight. They stood and glanced out at the view of the pastureland below, at the cows as they grazed one last time before the sun sank beneath the horizon.

"That's beautiful," Pearl said in a soft whisper. "So gorgeous."

The sight of the land he loved filled him with confidence. He knelt on one knee in front of her. Took her hand and gazed up at the woman he loved and wanted for his wife.

"I know we've both said whatever was going on between us couldn't last because you have dreams and I'm not leaving Colorado, but what if you built your boarding school here? I would help build the school and housing for the children.

"In the winter, I'd help teach young women how to shoot and ride and all the things they would never learn in the city. You could teach them how to be strong, independent young women who were in charge of their lives.

"I love you, Pearl Weare, for the woman you are. I want to walk through life with you by my side, loving me as I love you. Will you marry me?"

She stared at him and he could see her thinking everything through. Then she pulled him up, wrapping her arms around him and he knew she was going to tell him no. Colorado and Jesse would never be enough for Pearl. His chest ached from the pain.

"Oh God, I love you so much, Jesse. Yes, I will marry you."

He jumped and then he held her at arm's length. "You will?"

She laughed. "Yes, I want to marry you. For the first time in my life, I've found a man who takes me seriously and understands what I want. You've shown me the real love of a family and I want that with you. While I would have returned to Boston to build my school, sometimes the biggest changes start in the smallest places. I love you, Jesse McIntire, and want to build my life with you here in Colorado."

He slanted his mouth over hers, kissing her with a rush of fervor. She said yes and all he wanted was to take her to Denver and marry her. Her arms slid around him, and he thought it the most wonderful feeling in the world.

This time he would make certain his marriage worked. This time, he would do whatever it took to make Pearl happy and if that meant building her a school, then that's what he'd do.

Finally she stepped back and smiled at him. "The sun has set. It's soon going to be dark."

"Yeah, we better get back. I love you, Pearl."

She smiled. "How can the worst day end so wonderfully?"

He squeezed her. "Let's go home."

CHAPTER 15

*P*earl knew she'd made the right decision to marry Jesse. While she had wanted to return to Boston to confront her father and take over her trust fund, her heart had known she was meant to be here.

As they rode into the yard, she realized all the changes that would soon happen and smiled, eager to get started. Marry Jesse, start their life together, and build her school.

"I'll let you tell Grace and your father."

He shook his head. "We're telling them both together, now."

"Are you sure?"

"Grace needs to understand we're going to be a family. You're my wife, her new mother."

Grace did cry when she learned she was leaving and said she wanted her to be her mother, but did she mean it?

As soon as Jesse pulled the horse to a stop and slid off the back of the animal, he came around and lifted her down. She couldn't help but caress the side of his face.

"Now, Miss Weare, you're going to have to watch yourself before we get married."

She giggled. "Or what? Mr. McIntire."

Grace came running into the barn, followed closely by Cal and Edwina.

"Pa, you found her," she cried as she flung herself around Pearl. "I'm so sorry. I never thought about your horse following mine back to the ranch. I didn't know he was there until I rode up into the yard. I'm so, so sorry, Miss Weare. Please forgive me."

Pearl squeezed her tightly. How could she remain angry with the child? She'd made a foolish mistake that had changed Pearl's life. That brief scare had forced her and Jesse to realize their love and they'd compromised on their dreams so they could be together. He would help her with her school and Pearl would live in this beautiful country.

"I just didn't want you to leave," the child said as she sobbed.

"I'm okay, Grace. But your father and I have something to tell you."

She looked at Jesse and he smiled. "Grace, what if Miss Weare didn't leave? What if she stayed?"

Pearl couldn't hold back the smile as she glanced around at the people who really cared about her. This was her family, not those people back in Boston.

The child stopped and she leaned back from hugging Pearl to her father and then back to Pearl. "You're going to stay?"

Jesse looked at his daughter and then his father and Edwina. "Pearl has agreed to marry me."

Grace's eyes grew large and she clapped her hands together. "I'm getting a mother. And maybe a baby brother and sister. This is what I wanted."

Pearl glanced at Jesse and he looked at her and smiled. They hadn't talked about children, but there was the possibility of babies in their future.

Pearl's heart filled with love at the very idea of their own children. She would love Grace like her own, but it would be nice if they had others as well.

Cal cleared his throat. "Congratulations, son, Pearl. We're thrilled, but we have news of our own. Edwina has agreed to be my wife. We're getting married just as soon as I can get her to Denver."

Pearl jumped. "What? Edwina is this true?"

She smiled. "Yes, it is. He makes me happy."

Pearl ran to her aunt and hugged her. "You're happy? You're sure? You'd given up on men."

"I can't wait to marry Cal."

Jesse started laughing. "What a day."

Grace glanced at the adults. "Wait till I tell my friend Mary. She was bragging on a new mother. I'm getting a new mother *and* grandmother."

Pearl felt her heart swell with love. She'd come to Colorado as punishment and now she would never leave because here she'd found the true meaning of love and family. Here she would create a home with the man she loved.

"I think this calls for a celebration," Cal said. "Let's go to the house and have a toast."

"Grace and I will join you in just a few minutes," Jesse said.

Grace glanced at her father. "I'm going to get a spanking?"

"Yes, you are."

Pearl gazed at her future husband, hoping he would read her message, but knowing he had to do what he thought was right. "I'll meet you both at the big house."

As she walked away, she heard Grace say. "I know. I deserve a spanking. Let's get it over with."

Warmth filled her and she knew that while she hadn't wanted to come to Russell Gulch, it had been a blessing. This little suffragette had found a man who understood her desire to help young women achieve their dreams. And together they would spend their lives surrounded by the people who loved them and this gorgeous land. She'd never felt happier.

PEARL WAS HONORED to have her aunt at her side. They were having a double wedding. Edwina was marrying Cal and Jesse was marrying Pearl. The small town of Denver had turned out for the double wedding and the last two days had been filled with invitations, parties, and meeting so many new people. As she glanced inside the church, the pews were packed.

"I thought we were having a small wedding," Edwina said.

Pearl laughed. Grace walked in front of them in her new dress, carrying a basket of roses. "It's a big deal when people get married. It looks like the whole town of Russell Gulch and Denver is here."

Mrs. Garrison, the reverend's wife, made a clicking noise. "Ladies, of course, everyone is here. No one ever thought Jesse McIntire would ever marry again."

They reached the door of the small church and Pearl looked at Edwina. "Hey, you're getting married. Cal didn't stand you up or break the engagement. You're getting married."

Edwina laughed. "Thank God those other men turned me down. Cal is who I'm meant to marry. But look at you, Miss Suffragette. You're getting married."

A warm glow filled Pearl. "Yes, I am, and I have a daughter."

Grace smiled. "And I have a mother. And soon I'll have brothers and sisters."

Pearl's eyes widened and she hoped none of the people in church had heard Grace.

The music started playing. The three girls giggled and then came together for a hug.

"See you in front of the altar," Pearl said to Grace.

They watched as the little girl entered the church carrying her basket of roses and walking toward her father.

Edwina leaned over and whispered to Pearl. "Do you realize that if I get pregnant, your daughter will be its younger aunt and first cousin once removed?"

Pearl giggled. "Love you, Edwina. Let's marry those handsome men before they get away."

"Let's go."

❧

MICK MCINTIRE RODE his Appaloosa into Russell Gulch. He'd been gone far longer than he ever expected. Almost six years had passed since he rode away from his family. He'd been a wild, reckless young boy who thought he was a man only to learn the hard realities of life.

Pulling up in front of the Dry Gulch saloon, he slid down from his horse and glanced around at the town. It'd grown from a mere spot in the road to at least a village with a mercantile.

Walking into the darkened bar, he glanced around. "Where is everyone?"

Lillian Regan came around the bar. "Mick, great to see you. Why aren't you at the church?"

"Church? What are you talking about?"

The girl's eyes widened. "You don't know?" she said, licking her lips like she had something juicy to spit out. "Your brother and your father are in Denver getting married today."

"Well, I'll be."

But what they didn't know was that he came home because he'd ordered himself a mail-order bride. It was time he settled down for good and she would be arriving before the first snow fall. Could be an interesting winter.

Available art Your Favorite Retailer!

A Mail-Order Bride, Secrets, Lies, and a Christmas Miracle

Five Charleston women desperate for marriage-minded men and the chance to rebuild their lives after the Civil War answer an ad in the Groom's Gazette. Charity Kingston has to get out of Charleston or face life working in a brothel. But the past follows her to Angel Creek, Montana, revealing her Irish temper. And the bordello owner demands payment of her debt.

After leaving the military, Lewis Brown is given a chance at a new start in life. Taking a dead man's identity, he begins fresh as a saloon owner in Angel Creek. Imagine his surprise when a mail-order bride comes with the saloon. In a twist of fate, his past is exposed, his secrets revealed, and his worst nightmare confirmed.

Lewis and Charity need a Christmas Miracle.

Available at Your Favorite Retailer!

Also By Sylvia McDaniel

Western Historicals
A Hero's Heart
Second Chance Cowboy
Ethan

American Brides
**Katie: Bride of Virginia

Angel Creek Christmas Brides
**Charity
**Ginger
**Minnie
**Cora

Bad Girls of the West
Scandalous Sadie
Ravenous Rose
Tempting Tessa
Nellie's Redemption

The Burnett Brides Series
The Rancher Takes A Bride
The Outlaw Takes A Bride
The Marshal Takes A Bride
The Christmas Bride
Boxed Set

Lipstick and Lead Series
Desperate
Deadly
Dangerous

Daring
**Determined
Deceived
Defiant
Devious
Lipstick and Lead Box Set Books 1-4
Lipstick and Lead Box Set Books 5-9
Lipstick and Lead Box Set Books 1-9
**Quinlan's Quest

Mail Order Bride Tales
**A Brother's Betrayal
**Pearl
**Ace's Bride

Scandalous Suffragettes of the West
**Abigail
Bella
Mistletoe Scandal

Southern Historical Romance
A Scarlet Bride
**Belle

The Cuvier Women
Wronged
Betrayed
Beguiled
Boxed Set

The Debutante's of Durango
The Debutante's Scandal
The Debutante's Gamble
The Debutante's Revenge

The Debutante's Santa

** Denotes a sweet book.

**Want to learn about my new releases before anyone else?
Sign up for my New Book Alert at www.SylviaMcDaniel.com
and receive a complimentary book.**

USA Today Best-selling author, Sylvia McDaniel obviously has too much time on her hands. With over eighty western historical and contemporary romance novels, she spends most days torturing her characters. Bad boys deserve punishment and even good girls get into trouble. Always looking for the next plot twist, she's known for her sweet, funny, family-oriented romances.

Married to her best friend for over twenty-five years, they recently moved to the state of Colorado where they like to hike, and enjoy the beauty of the forest behind their home with their spoiled dachshunds Zeus and Bailey. (Zeus has his own column in her newsletter.)

Their grown son, still lives in Texas. An avid football watcher, she loves the Broncos and the Cowboys, especially when they're winning.

www.SylviaMcDaniel.com
Sylvia@SylviaMcDaniel.com
The End!